NORK
AND THE END

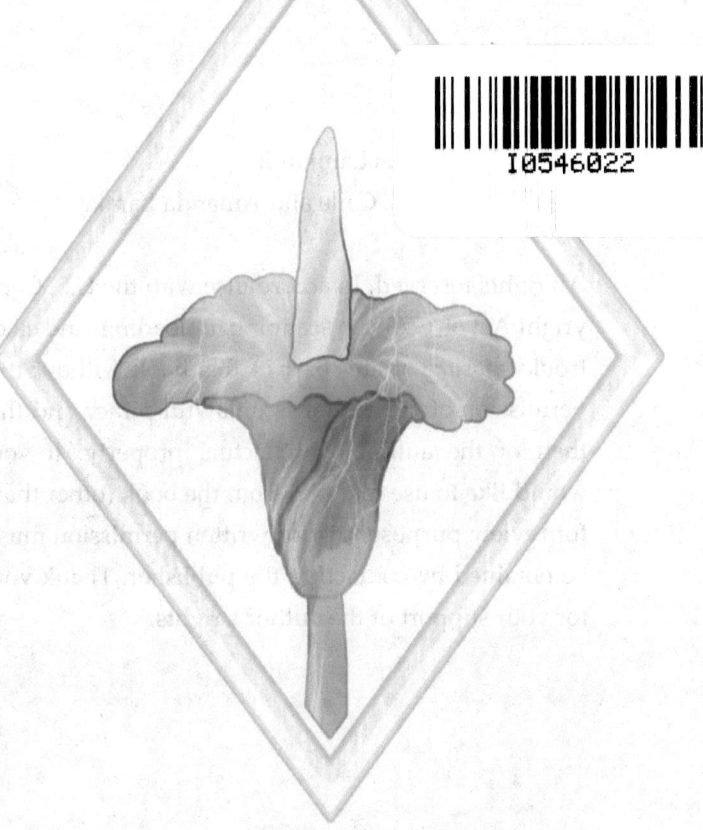

BY JAMES W YATES

-
- NORK AND THE END Copyright ©2022
- Line By Lion Publications
- www.pixelandpen.studio
-
- ISBN: 978-1-948807-35-7
-
-
- Cover Art:Thomas Lamkin Jr.
- Editing By Dani J. Caile and Amanda Lamkin
-

-
-
-
-

LINE BY LION
PUBLICATIONS

"But many of the priests and Levites and chiefs of the fathers, who were ancient men, that had seen the first house, when the foundation of this house was laid before their eyes, wept with a loud voice; and many shouted aloud for joy: 13 So that the people could not discern the noise of the shout of joy from the noise of the weeping of the people: for the people shouted with a loud shout, and the noise was heard afar off."

-from the Book of Ezra, Chapter 3

"Yeshua said,
I have thrown fire upon the world,
and look, I am watching till it blazes."

-from the Gospel of Thomas (Nag Hammadi codex)

EaR PLUGS

NORK woke up. No murmuring or key clatter came from outside his door. No footsteps, clearing throats, or bikes jerked past door frames to lug exercise enthusiasts to their day jobs. The commotion of morning simply didn't exist and this fact barely bothered Edgar Nork as he laid belly-up on his bed, letting his mind imagine that the rest of the world finally disappeared completely the minute he stopped looking.

He pressed his head back into the wall and felt no vibrations against his scalp. The pipes behind the drywall didn't stress as usual as they swallowed the shaves and showers of his neighbors. The morning felt clueless and creepy as the floor fan that shook its head "no" incessantly in the far corner.

He slid out of sweaty sheets, waddled over to his blinds, and yanked them open. The gigantic city looked sour in the far distance and still buzzed from the acid rain it drank the night before. Way beyond the sagebrush and polyethylene trees lining the other side of the rental park's retainment pond, he saw layer upon layer of infinite structure stretch to the verge of human seeing. Stacks of interwoven buildings blasted up from the dirt like some massive out-of-control plant. It all seemed made of the same basic gray thing. Nork smooshed his forehead against the distorted glass of the window and strained his allergic eyes to take it all in. He felt like an army of fire ants was ready to pry out of both pupils, but in the shadow of the size before him, the burning in his eyes became a whimper too quiet and insignificant to matter.

He got dressed after a long debate that ended in a refusal to shower. It was too much work getting clean. Instead, he reinvigorated his "Irish" coffee while watching the public park entrance across from his cabin where people would now and then appear out of the fog. He couldn't make out the grinding of bikes or the crunch of runners in the park gravel, and he found himself overdubbing peoples' cell phone dialog automatically with his brain's deaf dialect. The absence of ambient bird sounds from the overhead speakers left a footprint in his mind almost too large to see.

He turned back to bed and sat next to a bundle of blankets that swirled in the way restless nights arrange them. Scratching his swollen eyes, he let the fears rise right on schedule. Fears he relied on every day to help him navigate his own obsessive-compulsive world of sequence and routine. Each fear had a face. Some were old and gaunt and lost of their intensity. Some were smooth giant baby faces on the necks of fat bullies standing up tall in the theater of his mind, obscuring the projector show. As the host of these specters, he was responsible for accommodating each and every one of their needs. He could hear their disgruntled mouths snarling in unison and it made pressure in his ears, like being very deep underwater. There was an ache in his

ears, and he suddenly remembered. Feeling inside both
waxy corridors he removed two mustard-colored earplugs
that fattened in his palm like slugs.

PATIENT HISTORY

EDGAR Nork suffered nerves. Even by Nork's eighth year in school, he developed debilitating ticks that morphed into constant routine, so no one really seemed to notice when he left his desk twice an hour to go whisper mantras in the boy's bathroom while re-balancing his eyebrows in the mirror.

*　　*　　*

AS an adult, Nork's co-workers knew that he was prone to over-noticing. Those that worked directly under him hated him for that very reason. But none knew how deep the noticing went. During performance inspections, Nork called himself "attentive" and "detail-oriented," while appreciating the understatement. But this is not to say Edgar Nork was paranoid or schizophrenic. He never let himself connect dots over a conspiracy theorist's over-crowded map of the universe. He understood the world followed fairly simple sets of impersonal rules. The complexity he knew so well had little to do with dark political machines or distrust of the government. Nork's attention stayed micro in scale, comprised of the infinite texture of pure fact that existed around him. His mind magnetized every mundane detail so that the small and insignificant seemed alarming, and the menial became monstrous. In his small corner of the universe, Nork was aware of just about everything he didn't need to be aware of about the buildings on his path from the Personnel Receiving area to work: the condition of the emergency defibrillators on each office floor, the hinges of the bathroom stall doors, those that squeaked and those that did not. He even had expertise on the minuscule variations of his and other peoples' skin. Metzger, for example, the basement-breathed technical writer Nork washed hands with coincidentally in the bathroom on a weekly basis. Metzger had a nasty red infection festering under the thinning crescent of his left mustache. Nork spent a large amount of work time every day considering what would happen when Metzger finally shaved his facial hair completely and exhumed this scarlet mark of shame from beneath his nostril.

Nork knew every blemish, lump, red blister, or nick on anybody he saw on a semi-regular basis. It was knowledge he didn't really find bleak or demystifying. He tried not to think in these terms. The reality was a stinging bombardment of things you didn't want to see. If you didn't have your shelter up in time before the raining fleshy onslaught of this planet's astounding filth, then that was on you. Nork wondered sometimes whether this made someone immune to the effects of beauty, assuming beauty is what's left after you forgive the world for being so close and so personal. Nork held everything under disgusted gaze, even his aging wife who he was surprised to be finding so increasingly repulsive. This Sherlocking into the basic human muck that surrounds everything eventually ended his marriage. He predicted it many expensive brown bottles ago, that he would die alone in the most immaculate of deserts, forgetting what it was like to be a grudging member of the stinking wet and always growing world of men.

Even if things were different, what would Nork even see in the gleaming body of the world's most beautiful female specimen? A soft and somehow eternal sexual truth? Or an alien landscape of tapping veins, hardpan skin farmed by flocks of dust mites that chew the flakes around pores like starved cattle. The freakish processing power of Nork's brain outclassed his ability to emotionally parse the world causing any romance that may still writhe inside him to deteriorate into a drowned worm. The syndrome was incurable, maybe even genetic. An inability to relish pure sensation without the balk of inner criticism, and disgust toward the near and soiled. Nork thought about autism, neurotic hyperactivity and all the other shrink-wrapped problems burbled about on psychiatry brochures thrown his way by many twisted and concerned HR faces. But he would resist these categories, opting instead to believe that troubles of the mind were as case-by-case distinct as personal histories. Each one was a separate species with novel DNA, and he believed that if this was not clear to people, it must be because they weren't looking closely enough.

Nork thought back to his latest episode. The one that brought him here to this park-side cabin, outside the screaming reach of his angry wife and away from the god-forsaken downtown and its relentless noise. He let himself get too drunk at a birthday party only his wife was invited. She brought Nork along because it was the cordial and least awkward thing to do. The host stopped being fond of Nork a few months before the shindig when Nork mercilessly critiqued her horrid interior decorating during a neighborhood barbecue and said her perfume smelled like the expulsion of a bulldog's anal gland. Being the elephant in the room at the birthday party drove him to overindulge and he was soon pariah number one, flinging spit on faces during diatribes about organic spinach and chemtrails. When his wife brought him aside to chastise him, he began destroying every household item in the house he could get his hands on. Not necessarily out of malice, but more from a genuine child-like interest in discovering the secrets that existed inside that made these people better and more worthy of wealth and friends. The police were called and Nork reconvened his awareness at approximately 4:30 am in front of a poorly painted concrete wall bearing the graffiti of a half-man/half-pinball machine being paid handsomely by multiple fully erect customers for a ghastly kind of service that pinball man seemed cruelly designed for but reluctant to provide.

FaMILY HISTORY

NORK stumbled into the kitchen of his cabin and saw it was the way he left it. Drawers half open, piles of implements stacked in meticulous but pointlessly proportionate spacings. A fridge kept wastefully ajar, devoid of edible food. Nork didn't mind clutter as long as it was familiar and well-spaced. He had always kept his wife's house messy but optimistic, like a construction site. This habit contributed directly to the destruction of his love life. But he didn't much care. The short but still significant stint of time he spent suffering in the same domicile with a woman he forgot how to love smoldered past his eyes during the nights he spent jacking off on the toilet seat from 12 am-2 am, careful not to wake the wife as he fantasized not of other women, but of other lives.

He pulled himself away from his thoughts enough to start chipping off shards of an ancient cheese glued to the dishes in his sink. Portraits of his pre-20th century ancestors that filled his cabin chaperoned this activity. The pictures consumed the empty space on his walls like puzzle pieces close to completing some bigger picture, and they seemed to over-compensate for his total lack of furniture. They made his living environment seem more madhouse and serial killer-ish than it deserved, and this effect was amplified by the fact that a few of the portraits were stippled with Nork's blood.

The story is this. Park neighbors called in complaints

on an otherwise quiet Tuesday morning about loud television and shouting. Phil Plimp, the far too mild-mannered park manager, knocked lightly before letting himself in on a cross-legged figure hunched down on the floor, skin scraped cherry red, attacking the portraits in a fever and babbling something about Platonic forms. A screaming TV vibrated in its frame in the corner of the room as Nork used it to project the audio/visual signal of an old video camera that he scanned the portraits with as if the camera was some arcane inspection device that could uncover the true nature of what it was pointed at. When Phil asked in an unreasonably docile way what Nork thought he was doing, Nork replied that he was searching for flawlessness, that he had seen it and now it was gone. Phil was used to the outbursts that resulted when Nork addled his brain, entered an itching frenzy, and began searching for evidence of abstract concepts in household objects. But Phil's nearly infinite patience had a limit. This time he could hardly recognize Nork through the swollen mounds around his tenant's eyes, and Nork swatted at his intruder like a drunk. Nork was removed from the building into an ambulance, drawing a small crowd from nearby cabins. He whined as EMTs wrapped him in blankets and locked him into the back seat stretcher, Demerol needles fountaining. The private frustrations that could send someone plummeting at 4 AM before a Tuesday sunrise were a mystery to everyone looking on. Riddles trapped between each concerned and narrowing pair of eyes. Nork's slightly threatening existence was the amnesiac fascination his neighbors never quite remembered until half-asleep again in the dusty parking lot, hardly able to distinguish the scene from just another installment in a series of recurring dreams.

For all the images Nork kept of the branches in his family tree, he knew nothing about his actual genealogical roots. That information died with his mother before Nork was old enough to know her. She spent her entire life amassing the Nork family history. It was her obsession, and likely a compelling reason why she didn't marry Nork's biological father. Other reasons included the fact that the man was an asshole and that his last name meant something regrettable in Norwegian. If she hadn't died and left her son to state custody, she would have found many opportunities to teach her son about the importance of names and why they emerge the ways they do. Edgar Nork was never interested in going through the mountain of files she collected. They remained unsought and unopened in the city library where Nork donated them. But he still thought about the people in the portraits constantly, inventing his own connections to the stern-looking ancestors. They kept him grounded to a floor beneath his feet that he felt was becoming less and less solid all the time.

Nork stopped to admire the largest portrait on his walls. Three letters were engraved in the bottom frame, distinguishing the portrait from the others as the only one labeled without a full first and last name. The woman in the painting was not a Nork from what he could tell. The last initial belonged to no known family name on record that the Nork women married into and her appearance was distinctly "un-Nork". She lacked the trademarked potbelly and bat ears that were typical of the females in his family. His mother always reassured herself that it was a blessing the Nork family genes translated so sloppily into the female sex. She insisted that desperation and ruin followed beautiful women around like hungry dogs.

The mystery woman was by far the best-rendered painting in the collection, and Nork believed it to be the product of a kind of artist's love and obsession that he could only vaguely imagine. The painter captured the subject from an unusual isometric angle, so she appeared to be looking up and over her bare right shoulder. Her chin rested playfully on the lightly freckled smoothness there that was curtained by a falling bathrobe and rivers of caramel hair. One eye was visible, looking up at the man or woman recording her with a vulnerable desire that was almost fear. Nork saw perfection in this woman. Her curving, effortless bend was not an awkward sexualization. Instead, it spoke dizzying things about a moment inside her body and mind, as she considered whether to finish standing or keep leaning forward on one knee like a slender tree because it felt good to stretch her thighs and at the same time be admired. Nork stared into the deep center of her right viridian eye and saw an abundance of patterns emerging to give frame to her flawlessness. Her beauty spiraled out from the center of her pupils, forming a Fibonacci flower with her other features.

Her hair, like the multi-green eye, resisted the assignment of a single color. Like an oil-water mixture or something moving at night. She was Nork's treasured ghost, his protected wilderness that he could leave alone and spare from his constant impulse to dissect. He loved her intensely. Not with lust but with that private instinctual and rarely spoken of form of love we really only hold for ourselves, but that we can also project into the world if we so choose.

Nork would have stayed and stared at the portrait for several more hours if his alarm did not sound from his bedroom, informing him that the world and its responsibilities continued to exist despite his mind's absentia. He dressed, drank, and got in his car.

On his way to work his hangover slowly drowned in the rising tide of a fresh whiskey buzz. Back to the middle, he thought, where the molecules keep dancing. He gazed out of his driver's seat window at a drained landscape and remembered when the fields between cities were bright places that seemed to exist for their own reasons. As a child, he recalled feeling drawn to their sense of aloof separation. The trees, fields, and mustard flowers seemed oblivious back then to the human purposes that emerged from their design. Nork did not empathize. He assumed they were gullible to be so willing to be transformed. To take the names and forms men gave them. You could blame them for being cowards, for not resisting the imposition somehow. Nork wondered how he remembered the fields so clearly. No solid memories remained of those places or what took place within them.

Maybe a friendship made, a stolen cigarette smoked here and there. He wasn't sentimental about it, but he still felt sworn to those spaces and to the sense of recollection that almost felt carried to him from another person, as a tale told during a previous karmic cycle.

Nork changed the direction of his glance toward his commuter train, (the one he used to ride before his company car). It snaked down the tracks below the elevated superhighway that paved Nork's route to the big metal accident named Fraternity, Illinois. If it wasn't for his recent promotion, he would actually be able to get to work on time like all the lowly new hires riding the rails below him. He allowed himself a split second of nostalgia for his first years at the company before any real responsibility kept him from being monitored when he could almost disappear completely.

The highways into the city were poorly maintained and always congested. Multiple police checkpoints slowed things further, causing at least six predictable chain reactions of nervous braking. Nork snarled to himself at the idiocy of the gas-powered automobile. It was 2090 and people still burned oil to get to work in a packed crawl of controlled explosions. Herd animals, he thought, as his brain enviously imagined the train's supersonic path across a satellite view of the American Midwest. The earth probably looked less appealing now from above the stratosphere. Intergalactic passers-by, assuming they were vacationing types, would see continents that looked like ashtrays and oceans resembling puddles of puke from a party no wanted to clean up after. Maybe the Earth's ragged appearance would purchase sympathy? Or maybe the planet was just a tomb overwhelmed by a fungus of city lights, and maybe that would spare it from the more enterprising extraterrestrials when they finally came to case the place. If the world was yellowing and diseased, inevitably so were its people. No one would bother the lepers of the galaxy, Nork thought. HOPE© would keep it that way.

HOPE© (OR HEALTH OPTIONS POST-ENVIRONMENT)

NORK, along with 80% of the global workforce, worked at HOPE©: bringer of last medicine to the world's lepers. HOPE© was *the* developer, manufacturer, and distributor of all worldwide health solutions; devices, and medications that would eventually kill everyone and would therefore never reach the root of the problem unless the root of the problem was simply the human species. As the training slogan went, "Diseases must be cultivated." Not cured. Not like those trees, Nork thought, that are missing from the landscape outside his car window. Their purpose was addressed, and look how they disappeared. People need to be dragged around, the sick and paying ones, and that included everybody in the post-world. Surely being of no use to anyone before an early grave is worse than just dying. Nork shook his head to rattle the training, and knock it off its feet. He knew the world was sick with that, too. Bad ideas. And that was partly his fault. It was his job to be a vessel for well-articulated evil as Lead of Global Messaging (or "The Horse-Shitter Laureate" as his friend Dolden liked to call him) for Health Options Post-Environment. That occupational permission kept the cognitive dissonance at bay on mornings like these, as Nork watched the gray passing world inch closer and closer to pure black.

He thought seriously about whether his profession

was exploitative or immoral. Those were other words that mutated unrecognizably within the last century, he thought. Eighty years earlier in human history working for HOPE© would definitely be considered unethical, if not a complete human rights violation. But the rules changed and so did people's expectations about life. His work in Last-Gen pharmaceuticals was a silver lining for an already fading cloud. For the most part, people accepted a 30–40-year lifespan prognosis and a 90% chance of getting cancer and/or auto-immune disease by age 14. Besides, every for-profit industry has to at least try to be sustainable even if people can't be anymore. Maybe HOPE© Enterprises with its vast wingspan of world market dominance was the angel shepherding this planet's fading master species into the next spiritual dimension? Nork stopped for a second, thinking that this did not sound like his own idea and that it was probably spawned from his friend Dolden or an idyllic image displayed on a bathroom HOPE© ad. Nork then wondered about how many recent thoughts of his he could really call his *own,* and how much of his thinking was just uninspired briar growing out of the drug-soaked mulch of his shredded experiential record.

Nork pulled into the blue toothpaste-colored tunnel of the HOPE© Personnel Receiving area. He parked, got out of his car, and flagged down one of the Auto Valets loitering nearby.

"HOW CAN I HOWWWLP?" It said while slurring the last word through its spyware clogged operating system.

The service industry automatons were easy targets for hacks, with their not-so-subtle data ports located at the base of their spines. Any time a corporate spy wanted to use one for commercial surveillance or brand research, all it took was a good shivving with an inconspicuous flash drive. Hacker kids were always having their fun too, hence last month's report in City Lookout magazine about cross-dressing, self-effacing, foul-mouthed valet bots taking over the streets for a night of awkward metallic debauchery.

Nork dangled his car keys in front of the tired silver face in front of him. "Garage, please."

"HAPPY TO HOWL-L-L-L-P," it sniffled as tears of dirty lubricant formed at its faceplate seams.

Nork stood shaking his head as the pathetic thing tried to negotiate the curb beside his car. Each time it failed to bend its joints far enough to make it over the edge, it looked up at Nork with grinning apology, "kill me now" whispered somewhere inside the cave of its eyes. This was more evidence feeding Nork's belief that humanoid robots were wasteful trinkets that offered diminishing returns to society. HOPE© could save millions of dollars per year if they scrapped the electronic idiots and actually hired from the massive human unemployment pool. Humans were idiots, too, but at least their bodies were based loosely around a solid design. But maybe millions were just chump change. There couldn't be a single person or even a group of people that really knew everything or even cared about where HOPE©'s money was going. A company that owned everything *was* everything. The money just swam in circles like a big green shark devouring its own paper shit.

Nork joined a reluctant mob that filed out through the narrow aisle of a nearby commuter shuttle. Exiting the trains was a task easily overlooked when calculating the time required to get to work. Last year, HOPE© invested in new Polyfold™ trains with holding capacities that seemed paradoxical when looking at the vehicles from the outside. The things absorbed disproportionate amounts of people at residential boarding areas like long white clown cars. Upon entrance, passengers beheld the wonders of modern spatial design: four levels of seating collapsed into a plastic mausoleum of human filing cabinets. People bent into spine-compressed crescents to spoon en masse on their way to work as they watched highlights from the morning news smashed against their faces on the illuminated headrests of their neighbor's seat backing. People dislodged during each 20-minute exodus at the receiving area in infinite denial that anything about the process was humiliating. Through the porthole windows, Nork saw their teetering legs and thought instantly of a trapped Chinese festival dragon manned by the blind.

Nork collided through the packed personnel station like a misplaced molecule unconsciously seeking a working bond. He needed the Redwood 14 elevator that serviced the upper-mid office network. Most significant features of the HOPE© complex were named after extinct species or geographical features. It was a borrowed nostalgia that he found ridiculous. But all the same, each day's ascent in the mighty Redwood 14 found him hoping that cables would snap during the lift and that metal would twist open on secrets between floors. Each day it was a different archetypal landscape framed between sliding doors. Icy white forests, turquoise bays, cobwebbed crypts (depending on his mood). He would stand in that moment every swollen morning, savoring the effect this had on him and forgetting the permanence of objects for once in favor of his own private game of "peek-a-boo".

Nork's latest assignment located him in the center of "The HOPE© Tree," a phallic monolith of office space that rose from the receiving area up to the great white heavens. It was formed almost entirely out of puke green circus glass with spiraling grooves that made it look tacky like a cheap sex toy or a thinly blown marijuana pipe. His friend Dolden dubbed it the "Glitter-Prick" on his first day and the name stuck like it was screwed on.

Nork remembered an architecture class he took during college where his futurist instructor ranted for an hour every week about all the aesthetic disappointments of the post-world. The 1000-foot cock Nork climbed each day to work would be a prime object lesson for what his grim teacher considered to be the death of design in the late 21st century:

"Of course, alternative energy became huge at the tail end of the 2060s, (necessity being the mother), which coincided with a few unexpected advances in material science that gave just about every city in the civilized world a case of serious construction bulimia.

And here we have the new post-world city. Not the meticulous utopia science fiction visionaries dreamed of. Habitats and towns swallowed whole, badly digested, and thrown back up into hideous confetti. Meanwhile, the new century's economy only fattens a candy sandwich of corporate ephemera as our society of mediocrity oozes laterally, multiplying the same dumb infrastructure on top of itself. Every brick piled onto the mess gives ugliness richer nuance."

Nork considered his instructor to be a pessimistic dick, but couldn't help agreeing that the man was right. Tastes change direction but when they change too many times, they get disoriented. Sometimes not just disoriented but lost, and in their isolation turned ignorant and deranged.

Nork remembered the "doom and gloom" that was so popular during his college days. He soon was among the sad lot that expected the world's cities to be derelict within 50 years after fossil fuel went scarce and the environment as it was previously known breathed its last. How wrong all the liberal naysayers were. Cities ate and swelled into even more complicated giants, and nothing could curb it. Because ways to stay stupid and enormous were always found. Not through serendipity but through will. Belligerent blood-eyed animal will that stopped at nothing to keep expanding without a clue as to why.

Regardless of the underlying causes, ecological decay was what man really wanted all along. The deterioration of "the environment", or "that which was here before" brought the boost the global economy needed as if Mother Earth were a crutch and the only real obstacle in front of realizing man's true potential to construct his own artificial world of ultra-convenience. No longer addicted to the traditional forms of nature, a new healthcare-based commerce flourished and people had jobs. Old methods weren't needed. Not when crops could be produced indoors, and the atmosphere could be artificially stabilized to maintain a livable amount of ozone. Not when substances vaguely resembling "pork" and "beef" could be stitched together in labs or compacted out of insect species that still soldiered on out in the Big Gray. Any chemical need previously supplied by natural resources could be easily synthesized. Nature was like an old book that had already been read, summarized and retyped in plainer English. Nork remembered some of the students in his college class expressing disappointment at the "injustice" of the human trajectory. Nork always found the cheat amusing and laughed at how tall HOPE© would stand, the grand Glitter-Prick of modern healthcare unsheathed and shimmering high as if giving the finger to God himself. "Hey, we finally figured it all out, Big Guy."

More words from college past lit Nork's mind:

"Old ecosystems can be torn down to make room for mankind's epileptic paradise, but no escape plan is in place for the toppling structure of the human being. Of all investments in human progress, no real consideration has been paid to the inevitability that one day man's flesh will be obsolesced by the faster-accelerating hungers of the mind. The bottomless desire to expand consciousness no matter the physical costs and become

something greater than what we are: limited, addicted to body. In the meanwhile, anyway, people are making money. So, graduate happily."

Nork thought about how the personality of a city reflects the general soul of its population. How would he summarize his own beloved Fraternity, Illinois except with the same words deserved by all inland boroughs now forced into closer quarters by rising tides and national re-proportioning efforts: impulsive stockpiling for a nice and cushioned collapse.

OFFICE

NORK reached his office after a nut-shrinking elevator ride to the Department of Global Messaging that shared floors with the BioMed Solutions group of which Dolden Mastre was Principal Scientist. As Nork approached his own office, two of his Marketing underlings caught his scent and swarmed in. They cut him off at the hallway entrance closest to his door and unloaded the dump truck of their daily anxieties. They were blathering something about bad translations in the latest batch of prints for the new LUPUS PAL! Inflammation Management System that was slated for launch in Southeast Asia. Nork's lack of interest was almost painful. Every project at HOPE© was absurdly behind schedule. There was little to no management oversight for tasks on HOPE©'s great "Indispensable Chain", let alone the lower-level project milestones. When he was first promoted to his mid-level position in Global Messaging, he would have found it cute that entry-levels were despairing about translation hiccups. Now it was just pathetic. They weren't important enough to be fired. His underlings continued to vent and dismay as Nork noticed the slow approach of two Bird's Eye View managers from down the hall. The bosses walked stiffly but with pluck, almost on the tip of their toes as if pleased with the results from a recent colonoscopy. Nork saw the glint in their eyes. They seemed thirsty for the milk of passive-aggressive reprimand as their bobbing heads seemed to run together like some mythological bird. It was against all instinct not to consider them one and the same loathsome creature. "The Death Peckers," Nork sighed, borrowing Dolden's widely used phrase.

Just as Nork was preparing his defenses backed against the stucco, Dolden swooped in from a nearby office and intercepted the approach, "Hey guys, any word yet on the departmental report you owe me for BioMed? I don't mean to treat you guys like high school kids, but it's three days past due, and you're losing DETAILED RECOGNITION at spectacular rates…"

The slightly taller one spoke up, "Check your deliverables matrix again, Mr. Dolden, we have exactly one week before that task impacts the critical chain. Where is Mr. Nork…"

"Nork? What do you want with that useless bastard? Hey, speaking of you guys reminding me of kids. Do you guys ever go to camp? I've had this ridiculous camp song stuck in my head for days."

Both bosses were immediately sucked down the trap door of context loss.

"'If You're Happy and You Know It.' Have you ever considered the negative of that premise? Whether you could be happy and not know it? How could you even prove that you have knowledge of your own happiness? Is it possible to assemble the justifications, and the raw data to qualify belief in your own happiness as bona fide knowledge?" Dolden motioned to Nork with a subtle nod, encouraging him to take a lap around the corner while he had The Death Peckers distracted.

Dolden continued, "You wouldn't expect a kid's song to be epistemologically muddled, but maybe that's part of the joke?"

Dolden had weird ways of pulling rank. As a BioMed scientist, Dolden outclassed every level of the HOPE© management echelon. Not wishing to incur any further losses to their DETAILED RECOGNITION ratings, the two Bird's Eye View managers squawked something placating to Dolden, noticed Nork was missing from his office and turned back toward their nest of fluorescent lights and coffee breath somewhere in the belly of the Glacier National building.

Nork appeared around the corner when the coast was clear, "Well-timed, Dolden."

"You're welcome. Is that four times now you owe me? Sooner or later, you're going to have to start doing your job, before I run out of nonsense to throw at those morons."

"I'll buy today's bugs, quit bitching."

"Kidding, Nork. You know how much I love fucking with those two. They're like post-op Siamese twins that still share the same shriveled turd of a soul."

Dolden checked his nerdy oversized watch, "I have to get back to my interview room. My applicants await me, probably each sweating ice water by now. I'll see you at noon."

Dolden's potentials probably were sweating, Nork

thought, assuming he used his cruel environmental chamber trick again. Dolden was on a quest for the sublime BioMed lab assistant. Each round of interviews was becoming more extreme. He had a theory about interview tactics that yield the most important information about a person. He spent months developing a protocol that detailed his own custom methodology, which probably made him better qualified for interrogation than the entire Bird's Eye View Intelligence wing. This independent endeavor, along with other extracurricular accomplishments earned Dolden a kind of stardom among the Personnel Management department, which reigned supreme at HOPE©. This was a wise strategy because Dolden had work habits that made him not just an impolite nuisance at times, but an absolute terror. He was HOPE©'s exotic pet. Brilliant, beautiful, and more dangerous than anyone wanted to admit to themselves.

DR. CREAM

NORK stood awkwardly in his office for what seemed like an hour, feeling freeze-dried by the air conditioning that was blowing too strongly over his head. The wall of papers that circled his desk became no smaller, despite occasional half-assed potshots he made at processing them every 30 minutes or so.

At 10 am, he decided to take a piss. The bathroom on his office floor was near the HOPE© plastics assembly production floor, so oily smells drifted in through the vents constantly reminding Nork of the cabin he would visit as a young teen wandering around upstate New York during his surrogate father's business trips. Perhaps it was an immature cosmic joke that a fluorescent-lit foul-smelling bathroom at the end of the world made him feel nostalgic for rotting pine needles, boat engines, and mold.

Nork returned to his desk and sat with his mouth unsociably open, watching his office window snatch the khaki-colored rain out of the misty air and splatter it almost purposefully in the shapes of foreign countries. Each liquid blot shuddered before it slid down the glass in a sewage-hued worm trail. He knew there was something about the whole scene outside that pleased him. The white business park wasteland. The plaything cars and plaything people populating the streets. There was something in the whole picture about the ignorance of death and the disorder of heat. He wasn't exactly sure. Not being sure about anything was likely the side effect of the Kriadex, not to mention the Shade still singing in his head from the night before. But he knew, he thought, everybody knows that drugs are never as causal as they are indicted for. They merely introduce a condition and the mind is responsible for the rest.

Nork thought about his little pill stash back at the apartment and made a mental note to stock back up on the free Kriadex samples that waited in never-ending supply near every break room station in the HOPE© complex. HOPE© liked to keep their employees alleviated. A stressed worker was of no use to the company nor to themselves. Besides, most people by this time in human history stayed overmedicated simply to remain alive. The bloodstream of a typical HOPE© worker was probably not unlike the highway into the heart of the city. A colorful and congested artery that was at any given time one minor chemical error away from catastrophic failure.

Kriadex was about as controversial as Sweet N' Low, though Shade was a different story. Sure, it was registered and arguably legal but widespread knowledge of Nork's using would smear his already blemished reputation. It was a chic designer drug for young doom punks and astral projectionists. If word got out that Nork had a taste for the "Silver World," he would lose any hope of being taken seriously. He was already accustomed to feeling that every look from his colleagues was a judgment festooned with the shitty daisies of office manners. This wasn't far from the truth, because there were things to judge, such as the stained and wrinkled slacks he wore every day, the odd couple of moth-eaten shirts he cycled through each week, the occasional facial bruises, or the suspicious conjunctivitis. But none of this mattered right now to Nork. On a slow Shade come down there is no time for picking scabs of self-esteem or appeasing the inner panel of second guessers that hold the basic joys of life chronically on trial. He was too enamored by the depth of the world, witnessing the life cycles of raindrops on his window, or playing with the concept of object permanence in the elevator. How could he give a damn about the opinions of others when the vibration of his skin after a hot hand washing turned his entire body into one exquisite blur inside his clothes?

As he looked out over the commuter lanes, the cars, construction, and lunch-breaking human figurines, he wondered to himself how many people have had the occasion to feel a morning through Shade. He tried to imagine some brilliant way to persist the feeling. Find a way to preserve it and carry it forward beyond the trip and into the heavy and sweltering realm of the sober. He knew that he would always come back from the Shade just as bitter and longing, and maybe his fundamental doubt in the possibility of life was why.

After the Shade wore off completely, Nork sat at his desk straining his eyes through an allergic crust as he scanned over miles of text and let patterns dance in his vision like palimpsests of city lights. He imagined his brain elongating into a razor-sharp knife that was slowly turning in on itself. He checked his watch at 11:50 AM, had a drink, shot his upper thigh with a steroid injection, and went to lunch. On his way to the HOPE© cafeteria, he pondered the strangeness in the feeling of 1.5 hours of slack time lasting longer in his mind than a full day of focused work. His notion of time was doomed to this kind of torture because he swore that passion and money only mixed in a hypnotized self-help world that he did not live in.

Dolden was eating his lunch near the 20-foot-tall Dr. Cream soft-serve wall located dead center in the cafeteria. Dr. Cream offered the solace of milk sugar to lunch breakers postponing the death march back to their work terminals. Nork hated sitting near it because it was loud and colorful and a popular crossroads for people he wished to avoid. Each nozzle breathed a chill down his back when the lever was pulled by a chatting colleague with a jones for artificial sugar. Dolden preferred the frosty air and that's how it became their established haunt. Nork wondered if geniuses like Dolden had heightened body temperatures on average. If microprocessors needed fans to stave off melting, surely Dolden's brain required a cooling system that was up to the challenge. Nork wondered whether one day, as they sat chewing ant meat under the hobgoblin gaze of Dr. Cream, his friend would ignite with one final thought, overheat, and burst before his eyes.

"Nork," Dolden announced it categorically like one would acknowledge that it was raining.

"Dolden." Nork reciprocated.

Before Nork even sat down, Dolden launched into a painstaking recap of his most recent sexploits with his "girlfriend" of two years, the 99.5% robotic one he paid regularly not unlike a vending machine prostitute, though he would resent that comparison (The remaining 0.5% consisted of Dolden's various "bio-upgrades."). Each account of their relationship was uniquely disturbing, but Dolden had adjusted so thoroughly to an erotic relationship with an artificial woman that the tales of their couple's dynamics sometimes sounded normal. Still, Nork believed Dolden would benefit greatly in life from budgeting the amount of time he spent trolling around nightclubs for spare parts.

Dolden had a knack for romance. When he wasn't completely disgusting most (human) women, he was weirdly winning their attention. Then, when he inevitably got bored, he could wash years of intimacy off his hands like eraser dust and "go Blow-Bot®" without ever looking back. Nork looked at Dolden and felt his disgust and envy braid into one confusing knot of praise. Dolden was a dick and a complete fool but was so self-convinced that it was inspiring. It was a way of being that Nork knew he could never maintain himself.

"Rainin' out there like a promise broken by God," Their conversation was interrupted by Nork's former boss, Lesher Fixtrue, who had decided to stop by on his lunch hour. Visits from Lesher usually occurred weekly, when he wasn't in and out of hospital for his multiple weight-related complications.

"Lesher," Nork and Dolden announced in unison.

Lesher Fixtrue was the kind of fat that scoffed at the basic laws of physics. The man's frame wasn't particularly small, but his skeleton was outsized at least 10 to 1 by parachutes of flesh that billowed off his bones like oversized wedding dresses. He edged up close to Nork's seat, still standing with eyes dreaming into the gray outside the cafeteria windows. His hands grasped Nork's chair to unburden him of 50 or so surplus pounds. Nork could feel the rotten wind of Lesher's mouth-breathing sighs, and the infant-like convulsions of his sausage fingers as they brushed against Nork's upper back. Nork watched as the late morning coffee sweat stippled an elegant dot-matrix across their friend's pig-bone cheeks.

"Better be careful, guys, or you'll need an ark to get home!" Lesher huffed.

Nork was pretty certain it was raining harder under Lesher's gargantuan armpits than it was outside. The sole way Lesher seemed to know how to communicate was through biblical references and Sunday school puns. The man must have been a wunderkind evangelist in his youth, the kind that campaign around their high school distributing youth group invitations and borrowing out copies of Chicken Soup for the Teenage Soul. It was clear that his social development had at some point been stunted by religious trauma. Perhaps childhood epilepsy and grueling exorcisms by fundamentalist parents.

"Anyway, I'm being slaughtered," Dolden complained as Lesher continued to hover absentmindedly in their vicinity.

"Lifeboat," Nork whispered?

Dolden breathed deeply.

Turning his attention solely to Dolden, Nork began, "So they really trust the grand enigma Dolden Mastre with HOPE©'s Top initiative? How does it feel to be personally responsible for the salvation...ahem, eradication of the entire human race?"

"It's great. I can't wait to disappoint everyone."

"So, how bad is it? I have to market this project to our swell crew of Chinese investors so don't be stingy."

"You may be marketing nothing at all. I'm completely understaffed. BioMed doesn't have the resources to support this thing if we're gonna do it right. The pyramids were built because the Pharaohs had slaves. I need more than slaves, Norky. I need disciples."

"Hence your growing intern army?"

"Yeah, but it's going to take more than a fleet of green graduates to build Noah's fucking ark." Dolden glanced at Lesher to see if the rhetorical jab penetrated the fog of Lesher's daydream.

Dolden continued, "But, we've started. We're running genetic assimilation trials with our prototype right now. Should have results in a few months."

"Forgive me because I'm just one of the dumb word

guys, but it doesn't sound that hard, at least in principle, to reinvent the reproductive process. Don't you just need to find a suitable intermediary system to incubate and gestate human DNA? An artificial womb basically?"

"Oh yes, no problem at all to rehash a billion years of evolution. Wouldn't it be grand if the complexity of life stopped at principle? Don't be dense, Nork, there's tons more to it. Growth stimulation. Structural concerns. Quality of life. Brain function. X-factor after X-factor. And the testing, sweet Jesus the face-fucking testing. You should see our assessment protocols. The pages could double-coat the HOPE© Tree glitter prick like two giant paper condoms."

Nork snorted on a bite of a dry burger.

"Our new human needs life, but also a life worth living," quipped Dolden.

"Yeah, well, you should focus on basic mechanics first. Even if you can present a brain-dead human fish egg at the next Prospect Fair, people would count it a success. It's a step in the right direction. Eases people's anxiety about the Archives, too."

"We don't need steps. We need desperate leaps. In case you haven't noticed, we have a serious case of extinction going on here. Plus, we're running out of baby batter fast. Lifeboat alone threatens to suck up the world's last remaining supply of 'pre-post-world' sperm and eggs. The attacks on the Seed Libraries by those moronic Gehennist cultists are not helping."

Nork thought about Sara suddenly and made a note to

think about her again later when he was bored at his desk.

"Don't be so dramatic. People are still being born," Nork replied.

"Yeah, but the statistics are getting more and more depressing. Did you read last quarter's report? Life expectancy just dropped another 5 years. Infertility is spreading more rapidly, especially in East Asia. HOPE© can't keep humans alive forever. Not when the universe obviously wants us dead."

There was a pause. Nork anticipated a tirade that never came. Lesher finally sat down and started mainlining brown soup into his strangely small mouth. He had a way of stretching his lips into an elongated tube while eating, like an anteater. Nork figured he must be the last of his particular species, having devoured all the others.

"Well, at least there will be robots left behind to carry on some crude hard copy of our bipedal legacy on earth," mused Nork.

"Robots. What the fuck do they know? Vessels for our cultural bullshit maybe, but it ends there. It's not meaning to them. It's just information."

Nork countered, "Tell that to your aluminum girlfriend. Have you even tried to go human? At least once in the last couple years?"

"Don't knock BlowBot© until you've tried it, Nork. The technology there is...advancing." Dolden whistled suggestively as he pointed to a vague location below his waist.

"I guess we'll just have to wait until the savants at

HOPE© Entertains!© start churning out more Bill actors to have an intelligent conversation with AI. Maybe next time they'll dial in the personality to avoid creating another half-ton titanium teenager."

Bill was the first full-bodied incarnation of a humanoid artificial consciousness. Bill was also an actor. He was developed to robotically simulate complex human emotions, which became indispensable as the worldwide appetite for 24-hour soap operas grew beyond television networks' abilities to maintain a skeleton crew of actor look-alikes. The project was unexpectedly successful and Bill started being passed around the entertainment industry. As time went on, other actor-bots were designed but none were quite as expressive and popular as Bill. By the time the final refinements were made to Bill's design, he became basically a de facto member of the human race. People stopped thinking of him as "artificial" and more as a grand symbol of the coming technological age. All the vast possibilities of a neo-human species contained inside one charismatic celebrity. But Bill changed, as anything with a personality tends to do. His performances became increasingly over the top. He would burst into tears unpredictably, and seemed to lose the ability to moderate his expressions. He eventually became the poster child for that successful brand of ironic "bad" acting that carried many post-world comedians' careers. His crying mug shot became iconic. People loved poor sick sad Bill. The problem was that Bill behaved completely in earnest. After a year or so of being a worldwide laughing-stock, he stopped showing up to his filming sessions and public appearances and fell into a deep computerized depression. He was eventually discovered dead by his agent, having left a highly publicized note in his apartment before cutting the mainline to his plastic brain. Bill's note said "Try and bring me back, and I swear to God I will kill all of you." It was a huge hit.

"That fucker was hilarious. And a radical prototype for sure," Dolden remembered.

"Yeah, a foretaste of the future of suicidal androids," retorted Nork.

"Well, his suicide made sense though. That guy was hardwired to feel things probably 100 times more intensely than you or I. Built without the hardy little defense mechanisms that keep the 'bad thoughts' at bay. Maybe he just did what was logical. Maybe he saw things clearer than any of us."

"Do we need to keep you on suicide watch?" Nork inquired.

"Think about it, what made Bill any different than a human being except the depth of his commitment to feeling everything as massively as possible?"

"Well, his skin glistened like a waxed Cadillac, so I guess that's a start," replied Nork.

"Exactly, his constituent material. And, his origin. Of course, the origin of something determines the nature of its material."

Nork put on his mental seatbelt for the bumpy bullshit

ride ahead.

Dolden began, "I think the only real difference between the anima we observe in a robot, and the life we see in biological species' is about the origin. The material of the human being is painstakingly engineered by the processes of life on earth. Start with cooperative single-cell organisms. Then, the eventual growth of organs. A nose swimming through the primordial soup becomes a brain. That brain becomes a mirror. Consciousness invades nature like an army, and so on and so forth until we get too smart and kill ourselves off with our own mastery of the environment. Every aspect of our being is part of the same sinewy knitting, shaped by the constantly flexing muscle of evolution. Sure, in an abstract way machines inherit our evolutionary history, but not through the transmission of cells. They receive our cultural information, but the living language of our biology is not being 'born' into their circuits. This generates a translation gap. The language of our DNA has to be translated into binary code and shot across live wires. Something key is lost in that transfer."

"The pink gooey mess?"

Dolden ignored him and went on. "Machines are assembled and given 'life' by running current through inanimate parts. They are 'Frankensteined' from components manufactured at different places around the world, wired up and shot with electricity on an assembly line. They didn't evolve consciousness intimately alongside their substantive material for millions of years like we did. They cheated. Or *we* cheated for them. And as long as that is the case, there will always be a significant gulf between how humans and robots process the world around them because there is a fundamental difference in how the material of a human and the material of a robot is integrated with the consciousness that emerges from that material. I imagine Bill probably felt a bit lost, being bombarded by a world he didn't quite feel part of."

Nork stayed silent. He was getting tired of the conversation and was surprised by how mystical Dolden's argument was. Dolden had an extremely efficient schizophrenia operating inside him. There was Dolden the hard scientist, and Dolden the DIY philosopher. Nork wondered how his friend stayed sane with his worldviews playing endless tug-of-war.

Dolden began to muse, "It's too bad so much R&D goes into palliative healthcare these days, and not into the elusive biological essence that makes humans what we are. No one really cares anymore about how awesome the *homo sapien* really is, and how much time actually went into making us this way. There is a frightening amount of people willing to see all of that work come to an end. Most of them still believe all the work was half-assed during the latter half of The Sixth Day. Maybe that's why."

They both watched as Lesher slurped down the dregs of his stew, wiped his rubbery lips, and smiled vacantly. As Nork watched the goose-like contortions of Lesher's neck, he saw a strange tattoo barely showing above Lesher's shirt line.

An image of a heap on fire. Nork never noticed it before.

Dolden went on, "And maybe that's the model we followed for creating our machines: 'The Genesis Method'. The apple doesn't fall far from the tree, I guess. We have no time to take our time. We have to build Rome in Q2, the entire future in Q3. You want to see what really happens when you try to make a universe in 6 days? Bill happens."

Lesher burped, stood up, and went about the awkward process of adding Nork's and Dolden's dishes to his tray: "Well I'm headin' back, boys. I'll catch y'all tomorrow. Don't go working too hard!" He looked at Nork specifically when he said this.

After Lesher left, the cafeteria seemed quieter. The lunch crowd thinned to a few remaining stragglers.

After a bit, Dolden quietly fumed, "Fuck. Why does he always take our trays? It's like people that pay for things they shouldn't, or insist you cut them in line. Do we all have to be victims in their crusade for karma points?"

"I need a vacation." Nork choked on the last word by mistake, making him sound like he was about to cry. This briefly embarrassed him.

"I can put in a request for you. I'm close with our neighborly PR officer. And by 'close' I mean she's wrapped around my middle finger."

"Ok, forget it, you sick bastard."

"Alright, alright. Where are you going," Dolden inquired?

"New York. I think."

"Christ...," Dolden scolded.

"What?"

"You know what."

Nork replied, "It's none of your business, either way, I don't know why I even told you."

"Because you secretly need a sane person to tell you not to go. But of course, you've made up your mind, haven't you? For the love of God, don't get sucked in like the rest of those brainwashed tree-fuckers. You're not one of them. You know better."

"OF COURSE, BECAUSE DOLDEN KNOWS BEST," Nork aped using his best impression of the valet bot he encountered earlier that morning.

"Whatever. You're coming to my place tonight to get plane-crashed, right? New batch is in, and clearly one foul dude deserves another."

After returning to his office Nork fell asleep at his desk, worn out from the Shade and heavy ant steaks trudging through his sluggish bowels. Soon after closing his eyes, he opened his other pair of eyes that were closed on the other side, resting while he was awake. At first, all he saw was darkness. Then he was driving in his car. The windows were foggy and clouded. Dolden was in the passenger seat shaking his head. He was frustrated by something like he was having an argument with himself. Bright lights beamed on either side of the road the whole way, but there were no exits, so they remained out of reach. Like the suburb mansions Nork stood in awe of when he was young. Each one an impregnable fortress guarding someone else's entire life.

Nork's childhood revolved around New York like a small moon. His surrogate father traveled to the city routinely for work, bringing Nork irresponsibly along to explore the public transit system alone. Nork would ride the rails all day, exploring ethnic enclaves and browsing the gypsy junk for sale in the refugee tents that pimpled the public parks. He sometimes made it as far as the fortified walls surrounding outlying communities farther upstate. He would walk the perimeters of those hulking fences, hopping between stone slabs and looking for ways in. He had a fascination with the medieval-looking suburban strongholds, having been raised in a crowded city. He felt that the families that lived inside the walls must be powerful and dangerous. Far more interesting than his group of neutered urban hipster caretakers.

The sensations and brief relationships he had during these trips were some of his strongest parts of him and meant more than anything he had created, felt or learned in his adult years since. He hadn't been back since he was shipped off to school for corporate training. During college and the years that followed as he slaved at HOPE© like all the rest of his generation of state-groomed orphans, he lost belief in those old moments out of time. They seemed part of a life that was no longer relevant, like bright bursting years that had happened to somebody else. Maybe it was the drug of being young but Nork remembered a vastness of feeling during those days. As if his nerve lines formed an electric field around him that extended for miles. He wanted to see what was left of those places that once shined inside him. Most of all, he wanted to see Sara the Healer.

Dolden spoke from the passenger seat while facing away from Nork to peer into the shadow land outside the speeding car of this dingy dream: "New York. Never trust a tidal city. The air is caustic near the Atlantic. Inflames the brain. You have to do one thing for me, Nork if you go. You have to watch yourself around that bitch Sara. She's ruining everything I have worked for."

SHADE AND STORM

DOLDEN brewed his own Flanders-style ale in his parent's cellar and was probably way too proud about it. His recipe boasted quadruple yeast and absurdly expensive dark rock sugar imported from Westvleteren. Nork suddenly recalled an impression he had during the last drinking session with Dolden, of the sugar crystals bursting off of Dolden's shelves as if they were living spikes exploding out of a cavern wall. Dolden's beers were an unknown quantity.

At the end of each brewing cycle, it was customary for Nork and Dolden to share a pair of growlers throughout the span of a Thursday evening in the mildewed retro decor of Dolden's parent's basement. Sometimes they resorted to the porch if Dolden's mom was cleaning. There was something profoundly depressing about being drunk and 35 years old around Dolden's saintly and ancient parents. Maybe it was the kind but semi-insulting way that the Mastre's treated their son and his friend, offering them sweets and activities like it was just another Friday high school sleepover. Nork was repulsed by the regression this brought out in him. But he hadn't been "out" in a while and knew Dolden would just keep calling him until he caved.

Nork decided to take a walk in the park wastes before Dolden's. He hadn't really been outside in months, and he used to believe that if he went more than a week without seeing the sky that he would lose a certain grasp on reality.

A forgetting of place and origin. He wouldn't advertise beliefs like these anymore, but maybe he loved that they still influenced him.

The sky was charred gray and made him think of a dead stegosaurus being barbecued. Strange cuts of sunlight hacked through the black drift at evening angles. Nork searched for signs of a large breaking through stacked plates of reptilian armor burning on top of one another. He'd use the brightest section of the sky as his compass for the evening.

The longer he looked at the light in the clouds, the less he could resist reaching into his pocket for his pill container. The idea was already deeply planted in his mind that tripping on Shade would make his stroll much more interesting. Wandering the wastes on a powerful psychedelic was fitting anyway, he thought. Shade could do wild and vivid things to the radioactive oranges of a post-world sunset before the Silver World set in. The ocular nerve's last valiant grab for color before the world turns metal. As he shook two golden gel caps into his blotchy palms, he reminded himself that every action has an opposite and equal reaction. The ancient notion for this universal law is sacrifice, and Nork believed that a Shade user must retain an intimate grasp of that concept.

The Shade experience was not something easily described to a non-user. Nork tried to relate it to Dolden once, explaining that after the drug is fully absorbed the whole world turns metallic, glistening, barely moving and barely breathing. Like a winter without the cold. The Shader drifts like a ghost in the museum of the lost earth, all things encased in protective alloy. Like a private spiritual refugee, the only soul left in the universe and so briefly the only god.

The detachment from the social reality that Shade caused was so powerful that many users changed after taking it. The drug was not physically addictive, but there was a reason it was the drug of choice for many in the post-world. It was a total escape. An entirely immersive psychedelia. A drug that at high doses made other people disappear. Heavy shaders "saw" others, but not in the normal way, as other living entities. All normal empathic connections were severed. Shaders walked through crowds as if each person were a faceless gray statue. It was an ideal city-dweller's drug. A chance to cut connections to the human race for a precious 10 hours. Plus, it was a non-drowsy and cheap vacation that didn't require an inter-city pass.

Nork always told Dolden that what you take into the Silver World is the atom of self. The core of conscious life that makes some people willing to surrender everything in the name of a wonder that cannot be explained, and must only be touched for a split second before it is gone. Dolden always gave him shit for this.

Nork assembled his walking accouterments: gas mask, earbuds, HAZ gloves, cell phone set to "media device." His ears opened on familiar soundscapes. A promising start for a walk through a world that seemed to blaspheme in red, as if the air was wounded, bleeding and recklessly welcoming further attack. He entered the calm of his Shade ritual, easing into it like the twin pills sliding down his lower esophagus. He would have to promise himself that he never took them. He would have to fight back with that self-deception to carry him seamlessly into Silver.

After 10 minutes, he became a pair of bloodshot eyes. His face transformed into a pulsing engine for a nose that was newly haunted by the world. He walked toward the ground seemingly downward as well as forward, savoring his own weight from all sides. He could feel earth's gravity defining his body at its borders like he was being held in mercurial ink that sometimes blobbed outside of accustomed form. He felt composed of pressures he knew nothing about. Like a living rainstorm waking up far from home and feeling confused. He widened his eyes toward a canal, and toward the sludge lakes. The colors coming down over the wet acres were somehow involved in the music that swept through the tiny hairs inside his ears like trapped wind. And he was somehow too involved in all the color, breathing it in with exhilarated panic.

The Shade ushered him past familiar landmarks. There was stadium. There was copse of fake oak hemming in the bell tower that enforced the hour. There was the canal. Its water held insects and the last remaining world in hidden dimensions. The park's reflection extended everlastingly inside the water, and at the edges of the canal there was a folding between water and earth like two wings building parallel scenes into two distances: reflection and nonreflection. At that moment, the surrounding park seemed more vast and full of possibility than the rippled dream in the water's mirror.

A park bench near a lake arrived in his view but after it was in sight there were several lifetimes for Nork between the bench and every step. The seat was banana-colored and curved like a playground slide, the same yellow and the same shapes he associated with games of tag, bee stings, and static shocks on the tiny hairs of his stubby childhood legs. The whole thing reminisced for him like a ventriloquized memory. Like a disembodied thought. He didn't care how. Each vague recollection followed him like the silk of a spider you can't see close enough to swat from your skin.

He sat, took off his breathing mask, and grew into the seat in warm lines of satisfaction. Sun broke cloud and crisped on his arms, and he could smell the smell of himself. The odor caused by hours of being outside, sweating contently, netting in scents from the great swirl. That wonderful, confirming smell. Of a walked body. Proof of one's skin.

The bench belonged to an art park with ill-conceived pieces jutting out of the poisoned ground. None of the works really said anything. They were phallic, vaginal, or otherwise pointless. Sculpture, unfortunately, suffered the same fate as the rest of art's contemporary structures: in the post-world, the 1000-foot penis was king. Compensation through myth, Nork guessed, for the rampant infertility.

The bench that Nork sat on was another misfit

monolith in a sea of meaningless color and sexual posture. And it was definitely part of the genital conspiracy. He looked out toward the water in front of the bench. In the middle of the lake, a colossal stalk of asparagus rose toward the sky. Because the purpose of the asparagus was clearly lost even before the artist started the project, Nork ignored any possibility of clear artistic intention and instead tried to imagine how a lone asparagus could grow so large and so green in such a place. What bold acts of egoism were required to amass enough nutrients for this botanical freak to shoot up from the forsaken earth? He looked at the piece through the binoculars that were mounted on a viewing pedestal near the water's edge. A placard at the base of the stalk read "On behalf of Sara the Healer". Nork laughed. Had Sara's influence really spread this far? Were misguided sculptors seriously erecting enormous vegetable shrines in her name?

Sara…it had been so long since he'd seen her. He knew her movement had picked up significantly within the last 10 years. On several occasions, he had seen groups of her disciples disseminating pamphlets and performing their "planting" rituals in the streets of his neighborhood. Nork lost touch with Sara the summer before leaving for HOPE©'s corporate training. When he left, she harbored a kind of good-humored resentment toward him and his chosen path to join the "Death Cult of Modern Medicine." By that time, she was already on her way to starting a cult of her own. She had the magnetism necessary to be a spiritual leader, and

Nork often imagined her as a kind of glow-eyed demagogue even when she was still wearing her public school uniform and writing him flirtatious letters in her microscopic cursive. She had an air of occult authority that rattled Nork sometimes, his feet still firm on the sensible rug of Western thinking. She used this power of hers to assemble a group of loyal acolytes that began formalizing and distributing her teachings and methods. Nork suspected her influence was probably nationwide by this point. It was strange to him that she had become so influential. He didn't know how he would acknowledge her renown when he saw her again. He hoped desperately that it hadn't ruined her.

As he let his romantic nostalgia slowly take hold and smolder into self-loathing, lightning showed above the trees across the lake. Purple flashes interrupted the sky with a new frantic brightness. Like taking hits to the head, bad memories started impressing themselves into the soft mold of his awareness; club foot nightmares morphed into electric scars. The first spears reached at him from a collecting blackness across the trees on the south side of the lake. They looked like they were being hurled from a mouth, smelling out like tormented tongues of snakes. Searching, and soon to be zeroed in on the helpless rodent Nork.

Nork knew it was time to go but he found it difficult to separate himself from the yellow pedestal. Glued to the thing by the heaviness of Shade, he thought about dying while stuck like helpless bait in the honey of old dreams. During the span of time it took to consider a fitting closure to his life, he watched a white spike crack over the woods across the lake. He couldn't tell whether the blinding light had shot down from the clouds or stabbed up from the angered earth. The brightness burned into him, tattooing his after-vision, filling him with horror.

He galloped back to the canal in slow motion, the whole time feeling the speed of the storm fire up a fresh batch of fear in his stomach. It clambered up his entrails like basement stairs after a scare in the dark. Each thunderclap was more vicious, more canine, and closer to discovering his small slow-moving form beneath it. By the time the rain poured, Nork was trying his hardest to run. The Silver World engulfed him and clouded his muscular synapses as thoroughly as the storm now disrupted the sky. Dark rain hushed through the system of plastic leaves overhead, atomizing in a spray that obscured his perception of distance. Nork instantly felt selected to die as he bounded down the path to the canal, unaware of how ridiculous he looked trying to keep his footing in fresh mud. He could not move or think as fast as his panic could sink its teeth. He broke the polyethylene forest line and stopped at the canal. Behind him the clouds looked volcanic and cancerous, boiling fast. He continued along the canal path, terrified and frustrated by his impaired speed.

On the dwindling bridge paths, he saw no one, and this horrified him further. Nork's first rule of enduring thunderstorms was being in large spread-out groups of people. An evenly distributed crowd, he swore, helped diffuse the wrath of God. This was a strange intuition that always dodged his critical radar when he was in a state of panic.

Lightning was a Cliff Notes book for Nork's childhood fears: balloons popping at birthday parties, metal smarting on metal, exploding jack-in-the-boxes. They were all contained in that bright blue unpredictability that for some reason always felt targeted directly at him. He flinched under every flash in the sky, like each crash and peal spoke to him alone, warning him of its next path of least resistance into his spine. He could trace the history of the phobia through himself like everything else in his world. Objectively and godlike, like his own omniscient psychoanalyst, prying up the knotted root systems of his own overgrown psychosis. This was something he could not control any more than his mantras, repetitions, and ticks. It was a force as inevitable and inward-turning as the growth of his bones. And because Nork was his own god, he was not free. Because being a god of this kind was to be enslaved to having a mind and to the machinery of understanding. Like a sun surrounded by mirrors, he was trapped in the swelling heat of infinite self-reflection, frying in the microwaves of his own revolving light beams.

Finally, he reached the bridge that led back to the bell tower and stadium, on a road bearing toward Dolden's direction. After he was a moderate distance from the canal, he realized the needless risk he had just taken: sloshing through puddles under power lines next to a moving water source. He hadn't even considered the stupidity during his mad dash away from the art park. He thought about the giant asparagus, and how it might be faring now in the squall. He threw it out of his mind, letting the fear in enough to believe that the lightning could be searching into his thinking somehow. Maybe the huge metal vegetable was amplifying his thought signals? Would the lightning find him? Could it triangulate his position via the asparagus antenna? Maybe imagination is a good conductor, connecting thinker with subject. Maybe beautiful clairvoyant Sara could feel his fear from her high-rise headquarters in New York Level 2 as she slowly sipped her Salvia Divinorum and wandered the universe?

He felt more secure when he reached the stadium parking lot, amidst cars and rubber. The Shade wore off and he let himself slow down, still gulping air and fighting back the spasms in his lungs and shoulders. This was his body highlighting every day of wasted gym membership. Every bending night of drink-to-die he spent with Dolden. The same kind of night he intended to start as soon as he reached Dolden's and sampled the new product. This time it would feel more earned. Fear was a solid justification for alcohol. One he was familiar with. But Nork knew, knew even as it killed him that fear was a chronic disease steering his life like an all-powerful gale. And alcohol was effective. Temporary, but effective. Drugs are a utilitarian calculus.

Dolden's house showed up in a hiding mist that made every house seem connected to the other. A heavily bearded man sat cigar-puffing on his parent's porch, fingers contorted around the brown glass of a just-popped growler.

DOLDEN'S HOUSE

"AND there was Nork, conjured out of fog..." Dolden raised his palm dramatically upright in the air, in the universal gesture for 'conjuring,' Nork guessed. Nork walked up the steps, taking his mask off. He couldn't see it, but bright red patterns were showing on his head from the pressure of the mask.

"Nice tattoos," Dolden pointed at his own face for reference as he said this.

Sometimes Nork wasn't sure if he truly liked Dolden. They rarely connected in a way that wasn't coated in a kind of intimate hostility. They might not have shared the typical affection most people felt toward the friends in their lives, but they were both outliers in the same far-flung domain of the human resources landscape, and the shared status of being a tangential statistic approximated a "friendship" as closely as anything they were used to. Nork was grateful for it, but it still bothered him to be so close to a person he was sexually neutral with at his age.

Nork wasn't homosexual, but for some reason, his adult life was almost completely empty of women (except for his ex-wife who he barely counted). He couldn't help but feel ashamed of having close male friends at his age and hated going into public wrapped in that appearance. He knew he could fix this if he needed to. He wasn't hideous. Toxic at times, but not a complete beast. All his old friends from his early twenties had paired off, dug in, and shut down, just like everybody, just like he could never do with Sara. Nork had trouble with this instinct and he didn't fully understand why. He had powers of comprehension that he could apply with great effect to his own life, but his brain was still human and often hid things from him.

When he considered it, he attributed his sexual isolation to his own disillusionment. A real sob story, to be sure, and he saw the absurdity of it better than anyone. But with powers of comprehension come vulnerabilities to the demolitions of growing up. Nork knew how it sounded when he talked of a lost sexual mythology. He made this mistake many times over the years at parties. He sounded like a big pussy. It was impossible to achieve sympathy for all of his lost castles in the clouds, just like it was impossible to fully communicate the internal significance of a dream. So, he ultimately stopped trying.

It didn't help that seeking commiseration for the weight of the world was how he trained himself from early on to try and get laid. It didn't take long for Nork to realize the ineffectiveness of this approach. But by that time, he already confined himself to the perception of being a one-trick pony. He was a downer. And downers are famous for never finding the other downers.

Dolden brought Nork out of his revery, "Grab a drink, you weird bastard."

Nork phased out for a second. He had a habit of doing this whenever he first entered a conversation. Every ice-breaking comment he made set off spirals of involuntary analysis. Many of Nork's conversations ended at these points of departure.

"Are they in your serial killer fridge," Nork retorted?

Dolden stored his cornucopia of intoxicants in a giant walk-in cooler. It was a gift from his rich and oblivious parents when he turned 30. Dolden's relationship with his parents was always "ask and ye shall receive," even into adulthood when Dolden achieved a steady income and developed fairly antisocial habits. Greg and Giorgina Mastre had a bit of a weaning complex. Nork was surprised Dolden didn't milk this situation for more of what it was worth.

Nork returned to the rainy porch with a brown glass jug. A rich dark liquid sloshed inside of it, unfiltered and cloudy as the small rivers that were forming at the edges of Dolden's grassless lawn. Nork twisted off the cap, and the bottle exhaled perfumes of hops and fermentation. He breathed deeply. The rain's mists delivered the scent to the farthest reaches of his sinuses. It smelled complex but calming, like a well-articulated solution. He sat in the soaked porch chair across from Dolden and they drank in the rain.

Natural Man

THE two of them watched as winged insects bathed and mated in the algoid pools behind Dolden's column-raised house. The creatures flew with careful but improvised precision. They were so large it was easy to mistake them for birds.

"Look at those wasps," Dolden pointed. "Watch their flight patterns, the jazz artistry in their drinking ritual. What makes them any less beautiful or important than the bird species they replaced? Is it because we were used to seeing birds?"

Nork responded in his inebriated but still intelligible slur, "They're less beautiful because they superseded the birds with our help. They thrive because of us and the byproducts we've imposed. We killed the birds, and the stronger things survived. The stronger things are uglier and more dangerous."

Dolden looked at him, "You need to throw away this idea that man and nature are somehow separate and opposing forces. What argument could you possibly have to support the idea that man is not a force of nature shaping this planet every day?"

"Consciousness and freedom."

Dolden laughed, "Consciousness isn't unique. And freedom? Freedom is an inflated idea. We may be at the top of the ladder, but we still rely on the lower rungs to keep us there. Face it, Nork, we *are* nature looking right at itself, building and destroying. Even the trickeries of consciousness, the false dichotomy we create between man and nature could be serving some 'natural' purpose. The system becoming aware of itself does not change the fact that it is still the system. Everything happens according to plan."

"What PLAN?"

"The grand cosmic plan of cause and effect. Perpetually under construction. Always changing, always surprising. Plotline full of twists."

Nork countered, "So where's the responsibility? Do we get a moral pardon by saying that man is nature, and what's happening to this world is perfectly natural? You've glossed completely over our ethical responsibility to keep things from getting fucked up like they have."

"I'm saying there is something far more important than our entitled sense of morality. That every action, whether we see it as 'evil' or 'good' is a molding force on this planet that happens for highly specific reasons. We are just tools that somehow learned how to ask questions."

Nork exclaimed, "Oh, shit yeah, I've heard that before. Who was it...oh yeah, every major dictator throughout human history!"

"Yeah well, some people see things from a greater distance, at a much larger scale...and fuck! Pump the brakes for just one second here, who is this glassed-in romantic I'm seeing here? Unusual for you, Norkins, but I can relate. Who doesn't hunger for all our 'lost connections?' The small community. The farm-to-table living. The tribe? The ability to pine for the loss of life on earth is good because it is so pathetic. It means we are still human. You don't think I still want to cup fresh lake water in my hands? Eat real 100% beef again instead of rubber bug steak? Wouldn't it be grand to preserve the whole of folk wisdom in all its disorganized encyclopedia, right or wrong, and pass it down to my own flesh and blood? Let's resurrect the cooperative clan, bolster the nuclear family, donate our savings to those East Coast hippy seed worshippers."

Nork was surprised to find that he was getting angrier each time Dolden referenced Sara's cause.

Dolden went on, "Believe it or not, I am also still human. But what I want is to be something new."

"A digital ghost stored on cheap Chinese server space?"

Dolden smiled wryly at the reference to the Archives: "There should be a part of you that hunts down primitive thinking and drowns it in a bag, Nork. It's not always backward to desire a return to a past state of things. But it is backward to refuse to evolve. It's idiotic to separate man and nature. In all likelihood, the world spirit favors the new state of things, and that's why change is alive and humans are dying. That's why Lifeboat will be our comfortable purgatory. Those lucky enough to be archived will carry on our checkered legacy. Maybe this civilization of thoughtless destruction and reckless rebirth is essential to some cycle that's been in place longer than we dare to imagine. In any case, a dark part of me will always be curious to see what extent of excess is possible in this fat pimpled world of ours before it all goes down."

"You actually think evolution is moving us in the right direction? To the grave? Or at least cold digital storage. What if it's wrong?"

Dolden explained patiently and quietly, *"Can* it be wrong? I don't think there's anything right or wrong about it. It's just movement. The herd is migrating. And if you don't follow it, it will leave you behind."

The sentiments this conversation stirred in Nork were powerfully new for him. He lost interest in philosophizing about the old concepts of the "natural" world sometime during his late twenties. Exposure to corporate schooling, his group of jaded instructors and friends led him to demolish most notions about the world having unchanging sacred properties. There was nothing immortal about the farm. Nothing truly permanent about night and day. There was no science declaring that the natural world was and always would be OK the way it was. This was the time that most of America's agricultural production was shifting toward indoor hydroponics. Simulated daylight stopped the nutrient theft of nighttime. Advanced seed science eliminated yield loss and insect damage. There were a thousand things that were just waiting for humans to come along and do better. What imbecility did it require to imagine that things were better off without us?

During Nork's training days, there were thousands of

student groups that mobilized to defend against the mass technologizing of everything in response to the dwindling earth. Sara's Seeds cult was affiliated with most of them. The Cult of Gehenna stemmed from the same foment and they were definitely the most insane of all of them. Nork was taught to believe these people were radicals who were behind the times, and like most conservatives during that age, not to be taken seriously by good-thinking folk. They were pure atavists. A lost sentimental generation that believed unflinchingly in the intrinsic superiority of the past, idealizing an old regime that most of them were too young to have ever seen.

Maybe the destruction of the environment brought deconstruction of identity. If so, it was understandable that Gehennist youth were desperate for a sense of "creation", which became their concept of a lost home. Many of them were orphans anyway, just like Nork. They wanted the world to be something man could not make but had the power to destroy. Nork grew to see them as childish and in desperate need of something to react to. Maybe out of boredom. Maybe out of hearts that still bled freshly even though they were punctured long ago by someone or something very close to them, but still unrelated to the larger workings they so vehemently opposed. These kids represented the eternal impulse to have their own generational catastrophe that they could dramatize to their graves. Nork had moments when he wanted to join their cause, and write their manifestos for them so that at least their platform could be framed more respectably. It's a shame they were not more organized. They would have been taken more seriously. Sara, to her credit, always understood this.

As Nork grew older, he began to see that some of their ideas were a reasonable response to a world evolving at inappropriate speeds. Radical landscape transformation, new tech revolutions, and a deformed concept of human responsibility (what Dolden termed the "The Great Conscience Killing") were not inherently "bad". But they became problems when the rate at which the changes took place exceeded the ability for the majority of humans to rationally grasp the consequences and their own relationship to the events that ultimately ruined the world. There was no equitable distribution of understanding. No educational and social groundwork in place to prepare minds in time for the altered landscape. The flash information flood of the post-world. The sheer amount of confusion, possibilities, options, and answers suddenly made available to everyone finally defied any possible way to organize them effectively and show people where they stood in the midst of it all. This was the logical extent of ignorantly democratized technology. Meanwhile, most of humanity still needed to be told where to go. What to think. What to believe. Without that right amount of austerity needed to bring some clarity to the world, man became an autistic blob of pointless destiny only vaguely capable of comprehending where what, and why he ate, fucked, slept, and breathed.

It was the age of conscience death and the rise of ego. In his great confusion, man became parasitic, private, dangerously reinforced in the belief of cosmic favoritism. Nork realized that Sara's radicals were fighting for the right thing for the wrong reasons. They smelled something profoundly wrong. But like a drugged man confronted with real disaster, they could not articulate or fully anticipate the effects of the rapid transformation, the losing arms race of ethical reasoning against technological growth. They could only fight it blindly with wild fists.

One would have thought environmental collapse would bring widespread belt-tightening and renewed resource appreciation, but stupidity works in mysterious ways. After extremely efficient alternative energy sources were discovered basically by mistake, everything was allowed to become more abstract, disconnected, and post-modern on horse steroids. Communication systems crawled, bureaucracy metastasized, government vegetated and energy infrastructure stretched its nightmarish intestines of utilities and services until all aspects of life oozed slowly out of tubes like over-sugared soft serve.

"Why fret, Nork? The needs of man are well met during his slow slide toward annihilation. They are assembly-lined, per the eminent Dr. Cream model." Dolden summarized while bowing toward the beaming ceramic face of his parents' ice cream dispenser near them on the porch. Dr. Cream's benign expression showed that he agreed.

"How else are we expected to support dense population clusters after, and let's just call it what it is complete environmental apocalypse?"

Nork frowned, nervously unsure about whether 'complete' was an exaggeration or not.

Dolden proceeded, "I know. There's something deeply 'wrong' with it isn't there? But I suggest that you try considering that a good thing. Refusing change is like never growing up. You can't stay a kid forever. You can only hold on for so long."

Says the man-child who still lives in his parent's basement, Nork thought.

Throughout the conversation, Nork grew shaky with words of the world flickering around the borders of his mind. He realized with crystal certainty that the state of the earth really was wrong and Dolden was remiss to justify it from the armchair. The change, the dying, the world's creeping disease was pain. The scope was huge and the speed was juggernaut, and that was no bulletproof reason to embrace it.

VISIONS

AFTER their growlers, Nork reached that distance of thinking that visits during the body's first crude pass of alcohol breakdown. These moments were becoming rarer for Nork, having transitioned his alcohol use over the course of young adulthood from the occasional weekend binge to a slow, steady, and constant intake. But Nork was convinced there is always a window of time after the first bitter-sweet swallow, that may be shortened for practiced drinkers, where the world sighs and brightens. Within the first 1 to 5 minutes before the human brain releases its well-rehearsed defenses, significance is limitless, and personal impression is the only mountain in a 360-degree view of the universe. Every word must be released, as if its volcanic genius threatens to cool and be eternally forgotten.

Alcohol continued to have a powerful effect on Nork as the years passed. This effect he swore bordered on the psychotropic, but he rarely told this to anyone, because it was hard to describe what he meant and he sounded stupid. Nork wanted nothing less than to make the "drug" oversimplification available to explain his idiosyncrasies. This would bring no justice to him, nor to drugs. He wanted to fully own his reasons for being what he was. And Nork never considered himself an "alcoholic." A mug of Dolden's beer to Nork was essentially no different than Sara's mind-expanding tisanes. Plus, he completely disintegrated the profile of a typical drunk. Drinking balanced the nauseous equation of his conscious life, and refreshed his sense of placement in the universe. It even improved his relationships and may have been the sole source of all of them in fact. No demon is absolute.

He spent a long time considering why alcohol seemed to open worlds for him. His best guess was that alcohol functioned as a cognitive unifier, a kind of diplomat to the less cooperative enclaves that divided his hyperactive consciousness into regions of fears. When his inebriation centered within the optimal range of euphoria, he became nostalgic and borderline hallucinatory. A completely different world painted over the other one. And the new one was lush with an added dimension to things. More depth to the objects and people he perceived extended far into their substance, their meaning, and their minds. Each realm that rose out of Nork's drinking brain seemed truer than the world it covered, the world Nork left each time he stared holes into the blank walls of space, crashed through them and escaped. It became so that the actual world around him and the precise actions unfolding, taking him to each intoxicated moment; his hands, the bottle, the glass, the drink all lost their immediacy. Like flattened sediments miles underground, multi-layered foundations were allowing him to see from great heights.

Nork let his head fall back against Dolden's porch chair. The rain stopped, and the sky was whipped with breaking clouds. They formed a backdrop for a scurry of eye-floaters that twinkled and died as Nork's retinas swelled. The dreamscape came to him as he sat with neck craned, across from Dolden's talking shape, but outside of time. A world scene crackled into life, two-dimensionally at first as if appearing in fresh print from the clouds. Then boundaries grew and flooded the range of his perception with that same "extra-ness" and dimensionality that weaved and layered so much additional information into everything. And not just information, but intimate knowledge. Essence of things.

He was on his back in a hospital bed listening to two friends argue over something petty. The dream revealed no ages, but Nork sensed a teenager's mind inside him, blissfully underdeveloped and not fully aware of the devastation that was happening to his body. Nork was informed at age 7 that his game of degenerative roulette won him a form of rare rheumatoid periostitis. The disease visited regularly, causing his skeletal system to swell and ache and render him immobile. In the dream, he looked at his hands and immediately recognized the design of his dry knuckles and the pattern of papilloma warts on his thumb that was shaped like a map of Pangea. I am 17, he thought to himself. Nork's dreams often re-introduced him to his childhood illnesses, but his waking recollections of these days were hazy and almost nonexistent. Perhaps his mind dug holes into his subconscious and buried those days among dreams where they could do less harm. He always told himself that he didn't remember his really sick days simply because there was nothing special about what happened to him. When he was growing up, there were probably more bustling hospitals and care centers than fast-food restaurants. The world was sick. He never felt like he was special enough to justify brooding over it.

Sara came in not long after the tiff had started between his friends. What were they fighting about, he thought? It had been so long, he couldn't remember. He saw their lips move in the fluorescent light, just as he had seen 10 years in the past. From where he was resting, he could only make out one word. "Money," the lips said. Or was it "Mercy?"

Sara came to his bed. He could smell her perfumed wrists as they rested on his forehead. She was one day away from leaving school to start the Seeds movement in New York. It was gaining speed and now was the time she told him before. But she told him now that she would delay her trip and stay by his side until he recovered.

"If he recovers," one of his friends corrected bleakly with a chuckle.

Nork told Sara to leave and that he wasn't interested in anything anymore really. Nork said these words because he felt entitled to wallow in that special selfishness only allowed to the very ill. He wanted the pain of his moment of being forsaken by her. Besides, he knew she already made up her mind a week ago when she cashed in her academic stipend and bought a bus pass across the cadaverous countryside that stretched between Fraternity and the highest city on earth. Nork told her to leave and she did. Over the years, he would become severely addicted to this mistake.

"Anyway," Dolden was saying, "The desire for immortality is just fear of commitment."

Nork exploded out of his daydream like a diver low on air. He rubbed his cold eyes, wondering whether Dolden noticed his shivering, his nervous system still replaying the memory up and down his spine.

"All I'm really saying is when you finally reach a point where you have enough humility to stop expecting so much from everyone and everything, you realize that they really do give you a lot of time here." Dolden looked up into the gray-brown sky when he delivered the word "they" as if all along he had been a mystic priest of an ancient religion disguised in a lab coat.

"I think a lot, Norky." Dolden did a panorama with his lazily reclining eyes. "Living in this beautiful, once-in-a-universe still-life suburb. Looking at what we've done with this place. The things we've teased out of the landscape. Analogs of ourselves, monuments to our needs. What an animal can accomplish just given enough time. It's all so terrible and inspiring, it makes me disappear." Dolden flicked his skull. "A brain can lose a million cells and still be a brain. So, the notion of wasting MY life here, among everything else is laughable. It's obvious there's nothing really to waste."

Nork was busy trying to read the sincerity of Dolden's expression, waiting for the perverse punch line. That gracefully placed slur to rescue both of them from the ambush of authenticity. Dolden just stared forward after his pronouncement, as if completing the rest of the sentence in his head. Nork drank instinctively, tongue searching each tidal gulp for a feeling that had already receded and would have to be rediscovered another day.

CHURCH

NORK left HOPE© early the next day. His vacation was one day away and he was antsy. There was a careful mix of anger and awe in him as he drove away from work and watched the early afternoon hurl flames toward the city behind him. He saw the buildings catch almost all at once, watery and invincible though they seemed in the cloud light before noon. They conducted the sun like hot cathodes. All their glass made them appear molten and poised to flatten. The light gave him words without mercy as he drove, channeling into him a thousand different tongues. He let himself believe in the moment of genius as if it were another rare moment of "being in relation to the world". But he knew he would never remember the sentences that temporarily sparked his brain. They would fade like embers in the hours to come and become something old and out of context.

The surrounding vacuum of wilderness embraced the city and its concrete spikes, deepening their outline against an empty canvas, a flat baseline signal for the city's jagged pulse that spiked out of the blown static of Midwest expanse.

Noise.

There was a terrible noise to the city that was starting to diminish the further he drove. A constant underlying scream with a barely detectable low pitch oscillating inside of it. The sound hovered over the streets, humming like the half-angel charged with toppling every wall and splintering each pane of fogged glass. The note vibrated in Nork's skull. It wasn't music, but it was at least in its most basic form a consistent system of movement with no discernible melody. And so, the things it spoke were not spoken plainly. The sound confirmed every glimpse he ever had into what he usually described as an invincible fear inside him, telling him the tired story of the world's end he both welcomed and loathed. The word "end" was like flint over his gunpowder spine. A goosebump formed at each notion of total obliteration, bringing his life back, bringing everything back into focus.

As he eliminated the distance between him and the city melting behind him under showers of sunlight, memory harpooned him from both sides. Every beam of it carried volumes of information; details from being raised in the south boroughs. They seemed capable now of leading him on some eroded but confident path from his own blazing peculiarity to the universal place he desperately sought. For a split second as he raced toward the tall city in the east where Sara seemed to be hovering over the waters like a spirit, he was convinced some grand new thing was heading his way. All life looked expressible from within this isolated moment and felt miles away from the private beach of tongue-tied significance he'd been hiding on for so long.

For reasons unknown to him, Nork veered off the highway and drove to a chapel that was located near his old train route to work. The sun was just a weak sliver in the sky, but he could still see the place. His eyes were always drawn to it like all large tomb-like things that capture the darker verges of the imagination. It was because the building was old and was probably still old 100 years ago when the city was much farther away and the distance from the heart of the sprawl still afforded a buffer zone that kept the city invisible except for its glow.

The church was hulking and monolithic as if carved out of a single stone. To Nork, it represented obsolescence, but also a fetish for antiquated things and a marveling at how they persist despite the breaking down of everything around them. How did that resistance happen except by some spectacular power? He thought about the human brain when he saw the place and his mind started scrolling through trapped transcripts of conversations with Dolden. To Nork, the church looked like the first crude mound of reptilian neurons. A monument to man's first limbic clusters, still firing with first desires, visions of spirits, demons, and dreams of immortality. The "god organ." Still our foundation. Nork wanted that ancient spiral of lobes to be alive inside him somewhere, buried as it may be beneath a bloated and domineering cortex.

The church was seated on a rise that provided a view of the open space before the city started toward the northern horizon. He climbed the rock steps and wandered around the side of the building where an unkempt grotto overgrew and kept the place looking its age. There were graves there. The oldest cemetery stones had been buried in earth and now resembled early burial mounds. The grass on the mounds was new and Nork figured the soil had been deposited recently during the last major dustbowl that rearranged the Midwest countryside. These were post-world graves, he thought, drowning in a landscape of change. But some of the newer stones were still visible. Nork was glad people were still buried in the ground and commemorated with stone. He believed with certainty that the practice of proper burials would be one of the last things to leave from the human being. When that is gone that will be the sign, he guessed, that it was all over.

He returned to the entrance and walked through two huge red oak doors. Real oak, Nork noticed as he pushed them with both palms. Nork found a seat in the back of the sanctuary near a creaky fiberglass pipe organ with yellow stained keys that looked like fossilized teeth. The sound it croaked was prehistoric and beautiful, like a long-extinct animal come to life to lament eons of lost time. The pews were surprisingly packed. Nork wondered where everyone came from. Where was this barren countryside hiding all these people? The service began with a liturgy that was typical of the new generation of omni-denominational theology. Like all things human in the post-world, everything was blended and borrowed until satisfactorily unrecognizable.

The service continued with musical litanies, group prayers, and a trumpeting sermon. Nork was surprised as he looked down at his arms and saw hair follicles sticking straight up like miniature antennae like they sensed some strong signal was in the vicinity and were reaching up to receive it. When it came time for the Eucharist, the ushers approached the altar and fetched long poles from behind the pulpit. They affixed vinegar-soaked rags to the ends of the poles and swept them up and down the aisles of the sanctuary in front of the congregation's trembling lips. People leaned forward, eagerly slurping the sour liquid into their mouths. Nork watched astounded as if looking hard enough would let him access the ecstasy of egos liquefied into the great ocean of supernatural terror.

After the service, he walked out of the chapel, away from the chatter and sounds of catharsis. He was noticed but he spoke to no one. He remembered catching several pairs of dark eyes during his exit. The looks they gave were blank and opaque as black marble, but the marble was polished clean.

Outside, the night seemed so close to him he could feel it breathe. The sky was a low ceiling he could almost press with his hand and turn his palm black with soot. It seemed like he knew what he was going to do long before the decision entered his mind. That's the way it was for Nork during many of his Shade cravings. He still had 5 pills left, wrapped in aluminum foil inside his glove box. It was to be a legendary dose. "Why not?" he asked each pill as they burrowed into his stomach where they would prepare for an unprecedented assault on his mind.

THERE ARE STILL FISHERMEN

NORK had trouble identifying the precise moment he came to. The instant was smashed somewhere between the diminished snapshots of his slow re-sharpening awareness. His eyes shook away a blur and he heard bells. He was leaning against the steel of a canal. The air was burnt and sea-rotten. Smell, he noted, was the first grip on reality to return after a hard night of the drug Shade. The parapet he reclined against was covered in aquatic crust. The colors of his surroundings were oceanic and severe like the world was bleeding blue through a cracked calcium shell.

Fisherman bound a boat beneath his dangling feet. They walked imperfectly between docks, their heavy shadows following them, sometimes getting in their way. Nork wondered whether they handled each night's catch like the last slivers of earth, escorting white wedges ashore like the divvied-up corpse of Christ that they found floating out to sea. One of them smelled his hands.

"There are still fishermen?" Nork asked the ripe wind in his nose, bowing to its expertise. His senses did all of his thinking, and that's why a person without Shade over their eyes would have seen no one at all on the docks that morning. Not one fisherman.

New York

NORK knew he had ditched his last day at work and taken an overnight bullet to the canal district of New York City Level 1. He knew it but felt somewhat detached from the decision and from the flow of time that brought him there. With Shade still billowing up his brainstem, the action was saturated with a dangerous lack of agency. Nork knew this feeling was an illusion, but he also knew the platform of doubt he stood on every day did no more for his crippled life than a paper cane. He knew that in minutes a subway ride to the higher city would bring sleep and a huge square of heat in the sky, and nothing would keep it from becoming too white or blinding.

Already a city showed itself over his shoulder as some great and fragmented soul, surviving another night of crises and colliding. He grasped the city's scale in proportion to the bustling and lights of his own interior. The lamps he watched continue into dawn were also his, trapped inside his eyes, and they fought hard to the verges of usefulness under the assembling sky. The lamps seemed displeased about something; about the dream, they may have shared with Nork that night about disappearing. Having one last chance to jettison their light into the darkness as it moves aside for morning, knowing no lasting proof of their shine will be left behind.

Ten minutes later, he found the train he wanted and sat

smelling the rust of his seat as it took him closer to Healer Sara. From previous letters, he knew she was headquartered at the highest point of Manhattan, in a giant Roman Catholic cathedral that had been airlifted out of the smog of the lower levels and planted into one of the many skyscrapers where the rich and influential labored in their offices. Nork watched the city transform as the subway crossed the newspaper-thin membrane between city levels 1 and 2. Iron and brick replaced aluminum and stainless steel. Magazines that curled with dirty moisture on street merchant racks turned into large liquid crystal televisions, broadcasting essentially the same story, but with more color and urgency. The air itself cleared as he and his fellow morning passengers entered a zone where the purifiers weren't clogged from poor maintenance. Where people could breathe without masks if they wanted to, though it was still not advised.

As the train flew by Jumbotron after Jumbotron, Nork caught some of the morning's newscasts in the corner of his eye. The words "MASSIVE BREAKTHROUGH" pulsed across the scrolling marquis. A reporter was interviewing people at HOPE© about some new invention or product. He averted his eyes, wanting nothing less than to think about HOPE© right now and the mopes the news networks were sound-biting. Just before looking away, he thought he saw a familiar face on one of the last Jumbotrons that blurred by his window. It registered halfway in his brain, like a pock-marked neuron yelling across a barely audible gap to its desired connection. Was that Dolden? He asked very quietly, very unconsciously before forgetting what he saw entirely.

The only common element between city levels was the endless graffiti. New York became a canvas for the logos and obscurities of various anti-establishment splinter cults. Sara's peaceful Seeds were at the top of that pyramid, but smoldering somewhere beneath was the Cult of Gehenna. Worshippers of hell on earth. Nork caught a glimpse of one of their tags on a nearby building: the image of a giant burning heap of kids and the words "They will pass our children through the fire." Nork pretended to be unintimidated. His photographic memory from childhood Sunday School sessions in the city recalled a verse from Leviticus about that valley of slaughter known as Gehenna, something that went like "And thou shalt not let any of thy seed pass through the fire to Molech." There was plenty of that going on in the post-world. Dolden burned through enough "seed" in one day at HOPE© than probably the entire Bronze Age. But not in the name of that old dark god the Gehennists were so obsessed with. They were deranged. A belief system revolving around the notion that the apocalypse should have happened following the reign of the Roman Emperor Domitian in the first century AD. According to them, some Ammonite pact with the Molech deity 400 or so years before Domitian postponed the end of days until about "now-ish." The psychopaths craved the death of the world like something sweet on their tongues.

Nork pushed the graffiti and ominous references to

Semitic apocrypha out of his mind. He was already overwhelmingly nervous. What was he doing? He wasn't sure what he would say to Sara, or how he would explain why he was there. Maybe she knew already. Maybe she had seen it in one her trances. That would make it easier, he thought, because then she would own this strange situation about as much as him. He didn't even know if he'd be able to get in, or how her followers would receive him. He was after all a part of the enemy. Another drone of Last-Gen Pharma. But Nork still didn't quite know where he stood on the line between this worship of old and new. Her naturalists wanted to live and they wanted to die. They wanted to be members of earth, lost as the planet now seemed. Nork admired the honor in that. Everybody else just seemed to want to destroy everything or drift away.

In the time it took him to shake away the fear and the thousand visions of ways the visit could go wrong, he found himself at the hulking wooden door of Sara's Cathedral. The building was enormous and beautifully designed. A spiraling colonnade led up to the entrance, which was surrounded by a roofless atrium filled with crumbling sculptures of various saints and weeping women from some generally uncomfortable century long ago. Nork looked up at the imposing structure with his mouth agape. Two razor-sharp Gothic spires stabbed toward the clouds. Blue-tinted stained-glass windows spanned the towers like the eyes of a spider. There was a sense of finality around the place, like a point of no return. The door was less a door and more a one-way portal to a foreign dimension. The slab of wood used for the entrance was tall, old, and punctured with history, not unlike the crimson gateway to the "Church of the Vinegar Slurpers" whose passions he voyeured the night before. He didn't know where to go from here, because he hadn't planned that far. The Shade brought him to this place and now his guide was fading, deferring more and more to sober judgment as his brain stepped slowly out of its own haunted pool.

Just as he was turning around to find a drink someplace and think things over, he heard the whirring of a security camera above the door as it turned and focused in on his upturned face. It was too late. Someone would be down in no time to either greet him or shun him back to his own world. He knocked with flaccid hesitation, two limp knuckles against the impenetrable wood. It opened almost immediately and two thin sinewy men emerged from the shadows inside. They seemed to know more about why Nork was there than he did. Their eyes were white and wide. No trace of broken vessels. Their foreheads glistened with the residue of some oil that smelled holy like it had been burning for millennia. Nork followed them through a small empty narthex to an elevator as his guts boiled in panic. He was out of Kriadex and far-flung from the nearest star in his anesthetized little universe.

SaRa THe HeaLeR

THE elevator opened on a room that resembled an old gymnasium that was abandoned and overgrown with plant life. Small tawny workers flitted around growth plots harvesting odd fruits and primping leaves. Each time they looked up; their piercing white eyes prodded at Nork as if poking him on the ground with a long stick to see if he was still alive.

As he approached the far end of the sanctuary, a tall honey-skinned woman turned around to meet him. She stood tall under a large domed apse that flew over a repurposed altar space. The ceiling of the dome was gilded with some crumbling painting that may have been priceless at one point in time. Nork gazed at Sara. Her wrinkled nose resembled the skin of an almond. Something pressed upon by dual forces of growth and the stomping boot of post-world aging. But she had lost none of her prettiness. If anything, age magnified her best features. Nork could focus on very little except the infinite whiteness of her eyes. They seemed to actually glow with their own pearlescent light.

"Ah, Nork! It's been so long," Sara said through a smile that Nork had trouble looking at directly. "I hope Sagan and Tory didn't scare you. They see to my personal security as well as these gardens." She was referring to the wide-eyed men that took him in. "We have catching up to do, Nork! You want a tisane?" She looked behind her and motioned to one of her acolytes. "We have fresh vervain in our cultivars."

Nork scanned the walls again. The entire room was an arboretum of exotic plants and entheogenic herbs. The greenness and life in them made him uncomfortable. They seemed hungry as if they were reaching out to slowly embrace and strangle whatever came nearby.

"No, thanks, I'm..."

She looked him up and down before reclining in her chair and taking a sip from some steaming bitter drink. As if scanning the sputtering helixes of his DNA, she observed, "You're walking well. You look like you're in remission. What's your secret?"

"Luck, I suppose, and plenty of free drugs."

"That's right. HOPE© must not be stingy with their pharmaceuticals. I've seen you rise to the ranks of the Global Messaging department. You always thrived with words, didn't you?" She grinned sarcastically: "Honestly or dishonestly."

Nork's thoughts interrupted him. What did she mean by "seen?" Just what exactly could she see? His failures at home life? His weakness for Shade? Could her herbs and clairvoyance show her how broken a man he believed he became?

"The Death Cult of Modern Medicine marches on..." Nork smiled nervously as he finished his sentence.

Sara smiled graciously, and then her expression turned grave. "I have heard of this Lifeboat Initiative. It seems your good friend is spearheading the project. It's developing fast.

Faster than usual for a HOPE© project."

Nork nodded and wondered to himself how much she could know about HOPE©'s number one project. How many spies did she have lurking the halls of the HOPE© glitter prick? Or was there actually something to this astral projection shit Sara seemed disturbingly capable of? Could she travel the weird extensions and stand her cosmic form over Dolden's cluttered workstation as he labored to digitally archive the entire human race? This made Nork paranoid. He felt scared for the privacy of his own thoughts.

One of her acolytes stopped trimming a nearby foxglove plant to approach her and whisper something in her ear. Sara nodded.

"I have some business to attend to now. Why don't you come along? I can give you the grand tour. There's a lot I'd like to show you. If you'd like I can arrange a room for you to stay in during your time here. We have vacancies on the upper floors during the next few months."

"That...would be fine actually." He fumbled his speech as he became increasingly nervous.

"Come on," she urged, "it's time you learn our story."

CaTHEDRAL IN THE CLOUDS

SARA led the way into the deeper bowels of her basilica. Sagan and Tory trailed behind Nork, watching him with interest. They were not overtly threatening or suspicious. They seemed nice actually, but Nork was still deeply intimidated by them. It was their skin and their eyes. They beamed with unfamiliar health. Nork could smell the overwhelming stink of it. They emanated a dirt-streaked, plant-fed energy Nork could actually feel. It came straight out of their huge frost-white eyes. Meanwhile, Nork's allergies raged as they stepped through the orgy of exotic pollen flying around the facility. Sara glanced back to make sure Nork was keeping up. Her stride seemed faster than it should be given the distance between her feet.

"Keep up, Nork, I have something you need to see. Untruths are circulating about me and my cause. Maybe someday you can help dispel them. When we're ready."

They continued into a hallway attached to the right side of a large sunlit atrium that swirled with dust and plant spores. The hall led down to a series of chambers that Nork figured were originally used to house the bones of sacred men. Nork wondered what secrets Sara kept inside these mausoleums. She stopped at one of the entrances and swiped a key card down a heavily oxidized locking module that looked like it had grown out of the wall at some point. That's how every feature of the Cathedral seemed. As if nothing was installed or built. Everything, even the inanimate, grew out of some old iron seed.

Behind the door was a room filled with chemical equipment. It was a laboratory filled with shimmering silver machines that were at least 100 years old. Nork couldn't guess what purpose they served and did not ask. Sara led him past glass alembics, stills, and other alchemical obscura to a partition near the rear of the room. She parted a huge soft yellow curtain and Nork's eyes grew wide. Incubators extended almost as far as Nork could see through the crust in his eyes. Babies, alive fat and healthy writhed happily in each bed as nurse mothers tended to them, feeding them some grassy concoction out of mortars and pestles. Sara turned to Nork.

"This is *our* Lifeboat. What we've had years in the making."

"They're all...healthy?" Nork stuttered in amazement.

"Every last one," Sara exclaimed proudly.

Nork's heart began to beat fast as if for the first time since he was born like it was making up for a lifetime of hibernation. He looked down at his hands and watched his veins swell above his paper skin like worms surfacing in a rain.

"We've tested each one in our scanners. Their nucleotide structures are in perfect balance."

Nork walked over to a data monitor that showed a graphic of a double helix spinning on its axis. Below it was a spreadsheet filled with color-coded nodes representing molecules and bonds.

Upon reflecting on this data, Nork inquired, "Why are these flagged as errors? I thought you said the structures are perfect?"

"They are perfect. I guess a better way to put it is: they are balanced. We've spent a long time finding a formula for reproduction and nutrition that is synergistic with natural quirks. We have bloodlines. Breeders that can assimilate our botanical mixtures. We've found the fix, Nork. It's about flaws, properly proportioned. Like a balanced equation."

Nork was speechless.

Sara continued, "We were never meant to be 'perfect', Nork. Just in balance. Everything contributes to that balance. Every step of the process of life. We've micromanaged it into a reliable method. From sperm to egg. Zygote to fetus. We've re-written it like a piece of music that must be performed uniquely each time."

"How?" Nork was utterly amazed.

Sara sat down at one of the computer terminals and began calling up a routine. The computer display began scrolling numbers and symbols, so fast that Nork could only perceive it in his periphery. The longer he stared at the screen, the more he could see shapes and patterns emerge from the mathematical symbols that were too complex, dynamic and changing to call consistent. But there was a paradoxical property of repeatability Nork could clearly detect. It was like thousands of small rocks being dropped into water, causing an infinite dance of ripples and interactions.

"We call it 'The Song', and we're going to use it to rebuild this forsaken world."

Nork utterly surprised finally spoke, "Your computing systems can handle that kind of...complexity?"

"We were just as surprised as you about that. They honestly shouldn't be able to. In basic terms, the real sophistication of The Song algorithm lies in its profound simplicity.

Nork was lost.

Sara continued, "Far more complex DNA-matching equations we arrived at during the beginning fried these machines completely. But this one. There's something in it that self-persists despite processor limitations and random-access memory. For some reason, it's discovered a way to represent and suggest from the massive ocean of human genetic possibilities in some iterative, extremely efficient way. Our programmers didn't teach it to. It's as if it found its way to be simpler on its own."

As Nork continued to stare in wonder at the infinite scroll, he grew faint and nauseous. The endless spiraling in the code had so much terrible depth. A resolution he felt was tugging him into some sickening tailspin through deep space. It reminded him of the sludge lakes and the canal back home that he would stare himself into for hours, head warped on Shade.

Sara beamed at Nork. The pleasure she took in his seasick awe was almost sinister. Nork had no idea Sara had gone so far. From a cult of the lost earth to an actual cure for human extinction.

"This is real, Nork. This is life. Our salvation. And we are willing to protect it at all costs. That's why we cannot allow you to leave. I'm sorry. At least not yet."

Nork felt Tory's powerful arms cinch around his.

"What are you doing?"

Sara signaled to her bodyguards calmly with her eyes, and the last thing Nork sensed before sliding into wakeful oblivion was the smell of sweet smoke.

TIME LAPSE

IN the days that followed, Nork's perception of time changed with every thought. Sometimes speeding up, sometimes slowing down. Sometimes going backward. By mid-afternoon most days he paced the lodging that Sara provided, looking out over the high city and feeling the morning like a shell of himself he had long since sloughed off. Then his mind would take him to another place. Somewhere more painted and separate from what he knew, and the dawn that already passed felt so close he saw the softness of the sky behind his closed eyes. He thought about the longest day of his life. The day he left Sara for school and sensed the full weight of a decision he felt he was only partially involved in. As he remembered how her face ached in him that day, he watched the sun pause on its elliptical track as if considering whether to scoop the earth into its flames and bother with it no more.

In Sara's Cathedral, he found himself wandering a quiet landscape whose meaning seemed removed and protected somewhere in the past. As if the weight of his footfalls and the meaning of his breath were tied to some moment of brightness that came and went. At strange corners of these days, he found himself eclipsed by nostalgia so large and incapacitating, like a building behind his back but not touching. He couldn't quite grasp it. "Home" eluded him like a shadow burned into brick. He had only an outline of its old dimensions.

Before he even knocked, Sara invited him into her room with her strong voice from behind the iron door. Nork entered tentatively, so crowded with things to say that he became a balloon of silence. The words felt like they were transmuting because of the pressure, seeping from his tear ducts as his red eyes burned. He would never get used to this concentration of pollen. For a while he lingered near the entrance until Sara looked at him cock-eyed from behind her mug of Salvia.

"I don't...I don't know what I'm doing here," Nork began, "I feel strange. Like I've missed something. Like I'm sleeping too long, or not at all. I don't know...I feel like I need to go back to someplace. But then I also feel somehow like that would be the worst decision of my life. Another worst that I can keep reliving and reliving. I'm so sorry for..."

"You're experiencing time lapses, Ed. How long did you say you've been a Shade user? That's not something those street slingers tell you when they pass you those pills. Shade is the eater of time."

Nork inquired, "How long have I been here?"

Sara didn't answer, and this puzzled Nork. He felt like he had been under the influence of something his entire time in her Cathedral. Something slow and sharpening. Was it mental clarity now that invaded the rusted routines of his mind? Or were they drugging him with something? The uncertainty shivered through him.

Nork insisted, "How long..."

She stood up and glided toward him, interrupting him with a firm press of her lips against his. Time died again for Nork somewhere in the vagueness between their faces. In that crackling probability field between two colliding bodies dangerously close to becoming one all-powerful thing.

LIFEBOAT

"I heard it makes you cream your pants."

Dolden snickered to himself as he overheard this from a gaggle of Biomed engineers on his way back from the company cafeteria. They must be referring to the latest archival test subjects, he thought. Over the last few months, he observed that the process of archival sends the mind into a euphoric state similar to a heavy psychedelic. Dolden supposed the whole process was similar to having a rather pleasant near-death experience with a heart-shattering orgasm as a sort of bonus. He was curious to try it himself if it wasn't a one-way ticket and wished he could get into the actual heads of his test subjects to see what it was like. All he knew is that no one is archived without a smile on their face, and usually more than a smile. HOPE©'s board of directors officially documented the orgasm phenomenon as a bug. Dolden found it silly to consider it anything but a feature.

If only they knew how far Dolden had actually gone with his research. Would they shut it down? Or give him the Nobel prize? He didn't care. He was intent on seeing his secret Archon project to completion. Nork had been gone for close to a year which gave Dolden renewed (and sober) focus on his work. The amount he accomplished in just nine months astonished him when he considered it. Not only did he create an escape route for the human soul, a pathway to digital salvation in the consciousness Archives. He also created a shepherd to guide them there: the Nex.

For the last few years, Dolden used his influence at HOPE© to consolidate control over the cloning research labs. This afforded him the freedom and blissful lack of oversight to pursue his side project that he kept hidden even from Nork. The Archon Initiative. The creation of sterile genetically flawless humans to "watch the place after we are gone." Dolden wondered whether the Nex could accurately be called "human." It kind of did them a disservice not to consider them the next species in the never-ending sitcom of evolution. They were distinct enough and deserved a monumental reveal at the next HOPE© Prospect Fair. So instead of naming them something "science-y" like *homo sapien posterus* that would never stick, he settled on something simple. "Nex." Drop the "t," and make it hip.

In true Dolden fashion (and because secrecy kept him from recruiting other test subjects), he used his own DNA as the foundation for the Nex clones' biological structure. Each little test tube face was a photocopy of his. They were his children. His legacy on earth. When Dolden closed his eyes, he imagined the post-world flourishing with these wise homages to him. He would make sure the universe would never forget his image. Dolden the Father. Dolden the Creator.

He swiped his keycard and entered his laboratory where the infant clones slept in peaceful jars. As he walked down the lines of incubation chambers, he slid his fingertips over each cylindrical glass, stopping at the last one in the row. He peered in lovingly at his firstborn. Already, it was like looking into a mirror. Like staring at himself in the womb, every other feature nascent and undeveloped except the bizarrely identical adult face. During one of his nights of frenzy, Dolden named his first creation. There would be significance to him, he thought, as there is with every first. A piece of crudely torn masking tape attached to the glass read "Origen," written in black marker all-caps. The little guy would grow fast with the adrenal stimulants flowing into his veins. Dolden felt warm as he watched, dreaming of the day Origen first opened his eyes and saw his maker.

Dolden was so excited on his way home through the HOPE© receiving terminal that he could barely keep his thoughts straight, or walk in a straight line for that matter. Part of this was the celebratory whiskey he indulged in an hour before he clocked off. The other part was the anticipation that awaited the awakening of his first clone. In his drunkenness, he took the liberty of tripling the dose of overnight stimulants that would pump into Origen's baby veins. He wanted his son awake. It was time to start breeding his creations, teaching them, and making them as impressive as possible for the Prospect Fair that he knew he would take by storm.

The Nex were exactly what the stakeholders would want, he thought. Assurance of no man left behind when the day finally came for the complete crumbling of humanity. The clones were the supreme form of delegation. Archival would go so much smoother with them around to ease people into their goodbye chairs. Plus, the way Dolden engineered them made the Nex especially suited for being a healthy and powerful workforce. Dolden was already entertaining ideas for the opening line of his presentation: "Imagine if you will, ladies and gentleman, a world without sick days." He could already hear the "ooo's" and "ah's".

Dolden approached the curb of the valet area and found a lounging ValetBot resting its bolts against a nearby trash receptacle.

"Wake up, asshole." Dolden kicked the filthy guts of the aluminum golem. It shot awake; an apologetic expression immediately called up on its facial display.

"VERY SORRY, SIR. HOW CAN I HOWWWWLP?"

Dolden dangled his car keys in front of the automaton that struggled to rise under its own weight like a prize pig force-fed beyond the load-bearing limits of its legs.

"HAPPY TO HOWWWLP." The ValetBot scurried off to retrieve Dolden's car, tripping over the curb on its takeoff. Dolden swore he heard an "OOOOPS" as the mech recovered its balance and continued rolling away on its squeaky shopping cart wheels.

Dolden just stood under the valet area awning, shaking his head and longing for the day that polite and professional Nex clones brought him his vehicle instead of these useless junkers.

That night, for the first time in years, Dolden dreamed. It was birth. Or something like it. He couldn't breathe.

Not through the liquid in the flower, he was struggling out of. There was a smell. The smell of corpses. Prepared ones, surrounded in orchids. He punched his way out of a giant titan of a flower. Looking back, it resembled a pink fleshy tower that was now in need of serious repair. He was sticky and naked on the pavement floor of some vast arboretum. It was dark in the room, but he could see the shadows of other plants keeping their distance. Watching his every move. Everywhere was a hiding mist, a cloud that obscured his vision. When he caught his breath, he rose to his knees and looked down at his hands. They were aglow with blinding light. Each knuckle shimmering like a star.

It was then that he felt a presence. He saw nothing, but the feeling of "otherness" was overwhelming. It was a mother.

"Who's here?" he called out in a demanding tone. Stronger than he deserved to sound in his stripped and naked state.

All he heard was a feminine whisper: "*Look at your hands. That is my gift. You are The Lion of the World.*"

The cloud of mist grew thicker around him, and the presence of the mother became stronger. Dolden rose to his feet, hands still beaming with starlight. After a short time, he couldn't see a thing except for the flames of his palms.

The air was stale in Dolden's room when his eyes opened to morning. He stretched his legs and arms and felt the blood gush into his tingling flesh. He felt invigorated and stronger than he had in years. He exited the bed as if being lifted by a separate force. He dressed and left for work, too excited and scatterbrained for breakfast. His drive to HOPE© was desperate like a leap across a great chasm separating him from whatever had come alive inside his lab overnight. He wondered if Origen was awake yet. What would be his first words? Dolden knew he'd have to get there fast to be the first person his clone sees. He needed that initial imprinting to happen. It was essential.

Dolden slogged through the Personnel Receiving area and rocketed up the elevator to his lab floor. He spoke to no one, ignoring each blithering junior scientist as they dumped their doubts and data into his deaf ears. Finally, he reached his private lab, shut the door, and pulled the blinds. Almost afraid to turn around, he paused for a second. He heard breathing behind him. Calm breath through the nose, an associated heart rate probably swinging around 40-50 BPM.

"Hello." A mature pleasant voice said. *His* voice said.

Dolden turned around and saw an exact copy of himself standing naked on the linoleum floor of his lab. Clear nutrient-enriched goo slid down Origen's pale skin. Dolden noticed some blood mixed in with the incubation fluid. The clone must have cut himself on his way out of the glass. Either that or Dolden overshot the stimulant dosage and the jar popped in the night like a shaken soda can.

Dolden stuttered a bit: "H-Hi there. I'm Dolden. Do you...Do you know who you are?"

His creation spoke, "There was an alphabetical label adhered to my growth chamber. I believe the word was 'Origen.' Is that what you would like to call me?"

Dolden smiled, "Yes. You are Origen. That's excellent. Excellent. I am a scientist here at HOPE©. It's a company, or a government really. Anyway, I brought you into this world you are seeing right now. How do you feel?"

"Acute nausea at first, followed by some muscle spasming which I addressed with a 25mg injection of intravenous Flexeril and two capsules of Phenergan you had in your desk. I then felt sleepy so I rested. Curiously, my mind kept showing me pictures even though my body was inert. It was a strangely pleasant and energizing experience. What I guess you'd call a 'nap.'"

He's smart, Dolden thought, *and learning fast. Just as he was engineered, his language centers are almost fully formed already. He's making connections every second.*

"You must be hungry, Origen. Let me get you some food and I'll...clean up those wounds for you." Dolden began scrambling around his lab collecting a handful of energy bars, bottles of purified water, and disinfectant.

"Yes, I noticed some of my fluids escaping. I planned to address that just as you entered the room and introduced yourself."

"Please, have a seat and help yourself to these." Dolden dumped the snacks on the table, kneeled next to his firstborn creation and began salving the cuts on Origen's arms as the clone politely ate his energy bars and guzzled bottle after bottle of water.

Origen mused, "You have the same, right? Within you?"

Dolden didn't understand at first.

Origen perceived his father's confusion and swept up a glob of his own blood with his forefinger, "This."

"Yes, that's right."

"We have the same appearance, too. I saw in the mirror," remarked Origen.

"Yes. That's right. Do you know why?" Dolden paused and looked at Origen's eyes, watching the almost mechanical process of self-conception unfold within his son for the first time.

"Because I am a clone of you. My body contains identical DNA. I was created in those machines through a scientific process that you derived from existing genetic engineering technology. But I am also a distinct being exposed to my environment and constantly being shaped by it. Therefore, we are not the same."

"No, we are not the same," Dolden agreed.

"My genetic structure is also engineered to be perfect and free of undesirable mutation. I will thus live much longer than you and be free of what you call 'disease.'"

Dolden smiled again. Wider this time as he sponged up his son's miraculous blood and crisscrossed bandages over the fresh cuts. Dolden sensed the impulse within himself to consume the blood. To taste a god. Origen knew so much already. There would be less teaching needed than he thought.

Origen continued, "Another drive I notice in me is a notion of not just being here, but a need to understand what I am designed to do here. I believe I am here to live and to help. Is that accurate?"

"It is."

Origen added, "And you, and the rest that are unlike me. You are designed to die."

Dolden's smile lost some of its altitudes. He continued cleaning the feeding fluid off of Origen's skin and found his son some clothes. Origen continued to talk for hours, and Dolden just listened occasionally offering confirmation but mostly staying quiet.

After setting Origen up with everything he needed for daily self-care, Dolden excused himself. He listened to Origen verbally construct the world for over five hours, and found himself devastatingly tired, even a little sick. There was a spinning pearl of nausea forming in the pit of his stomach and he felt the immediate need to leave. He didn't quite understand why.

"Origen?"

"Yes?" Origen looked up from the lab instruments he was studying with infinite compassion and interest in what Dolden had to say.

"I'm leaving now. For the day. I'll be back tomorrow, OK? You stay here, understood? The lab is at your disposal. I'm sure you'll figure everything out." Some envy grew in Dolden as he thought of the entire lifetime of scientific knowledge that was gifted into Origen's neurons. The privilege inexplicably angered him.

"Of course! Have a good rest of your evening. Oh, and one more question if you don't mind..."

"Sure."

"What should I call you? I could default to 'father' or 'dad' if it is appropriate. I feel using your christened name offends my sensibilities and your cultural traditions. The word 'dad' also encapsulates our relationship rather well I think and avoids the more arch and religiously-tinged nomenclature such as 'creator' or 'maker.'"

"'Dad' is...fine Origen. I'll see you later."

Dolden left HOPE© in a hurry. Questions were waiting for him from almost every angle on his way out. Scientists and managers perplexed by the new sounds and movement coming from Dolden's private lab. He ignored all of their prattling mouths and continued cutting a path through the crowd. He wanted desperately to be alone in his car, flying away from this place at the speed of light.

Dolden's mind was blank on his way out of the HOPE© commuter district, as he sped across the open highway toward home. But there was a soup of feelings simmering in his gut, changing properties each time his heart applied more heat. First, it was a wide sense of emptiness, then nausea, then anger, then a profound regret that seemed to smash into his ribs out of nowhere. He'd finally done it. Completed his mission. The Archon project was more successful than he was prepared for. In the process, he realized he'd snatched from the forbidden tree. Discovered immortality, but not for mankind. The Nex would outrun humanity in a matter of weeks in almost every aspect of life.

"Designed to die." *Cocky little prick. But he's right. I've doomed us,* Dolden thought as his knuckles turned white against the steering wheel. They seemed to glow in the sunlight. *I'm the antichrist for Christ's sake!* He laughed darkly. *The Lion. The Blind God to blast the world...what the fuck have I done?*

Dolden drove fast in the same lane for the rest of the afternoon, overshooting his exit mile after mile, missing Nork and last year so much his heart felt like it was climbing up his throat trying to get out at all costs.

RELICS

AFTER his time with Sara, Nork wandered back to the elevators to return to his room. The upper floors of Sara's Cathedral were empty except for a few workers tasked with janitorial duties. Nork wasn't sure what time it was and decided he wouldn't know until reaching his apartment and staring blankly into the city's jagged face. If that face was bright and electric, it was night. If not, then the post-world sun was out pummeling the buildings into submission.

He separated the curtains hanging over his giant windows. The city was lit like the sun, but the sun was nowhere to be found. He studied the intricate tapestry of graffiti that stretched itself over Manhattan. New York was a nocturnal animal, skin covered in tattoos, a place where ideas converged to hunt at night and sleep during business hours. The ideograms, murals, and tags were phosphorescent under the artificial light. Gehennist, Seed, AI-worship, garden-variety Christian, they were all represented in the puke of proselytism. Staring right back at him from the center of his view was a strikingly well-painted image of a little girl holding a deflated balloon that was planet earth, crying tears of blood. Her skin was peeled off on one side of her face, exposing a robotic eye and metal jawbone. "THEIR WORM DOES NOT DIE" was etched in black above the child. Definitely Gehennist, Nork said dismissively to himself as he looked away from the girl before she looked too far into him.

He checked the calendar in the kitchen and noticed the date was several days later than he thought. He rubbed his head, too exhausted and emptied from Sara to find this significant loss of time unnerving enough to panic. He decided to go to bed.

Nork had a dream that night. The kind that picks up where previous ones leave off, as if the brain is never finished making revisions to a picture it desperately wants itself to see. Nork was back in his car driving with Dolden across the wasteland. The sun rose and set in the sky over and over again cartoonishly in a fast-motion montage. The city lights stayed still behind them like a permanent backdrop and didn't seem to get any further away. Dolden was talking about something, but Nork wasn't paying attention. He couldn't concentrate on anything but an extremely uncomfortable sensation that his entire body was hard as marble. Every time he tried to think or move, he was a rock colliding with pavement. About to smash to pieces. The feeling of impact reverberated in and through him like he was trapped inside a giant clamoring bell. Out of nowhere, two hands reached forward from the backseat and gently covered his eyes. Despite his rock-numb skin, he could feel the sandpaper calluses on the fingers that blinded him. Sara's hands. He heard faint yelling on the other side of those hands. Dolden roaring about a crash or something. It wasn't important. All that was important was the tickling in his ear of Sara's calm breath that dissipated into his blood like a cure for being made of stone. He was liquid again. Flesh. And the power words that whispered through his molten heart were: "No One."

When Nork awoke, his eyes darted to the door. In his peripheral vision he swore he saw someone or something quickly slipping out of his room. It could have been the smoky sheen over his irritated eyes playing tricks on him. Or maybe he was still half-asleep. He laid his head back down on the pillow, relieved to be awake and away from a black dream that now felt like a heavy closed bag he would never be able to reopen. He dropped it into the river of his mind, and it floated away downstream until completely out of sight.

Nork got up and slowly paced the room, unsure of how to start his day. He looked out his window and saw that it was still dark. The primitive clock in the kitchen read 6:14. He wasn't sure if it was AM or PM. Had he really slept through the whole next day? Sara warned him about time-slipping on the Shade detox. He wondered in fear how long the symptoms would last. As the drowsiness of waking started to succumb to anxiety, he realized he was desperately hungry. After getting dressed he walked into the kitchenette appended to his lodging space and opened the fridge. A blast of rotting stench filled his face and he nearly gagged. Every last piece of food, including the vegetables from Sara's gardens that were given to him just days ago, was severely decomposed.

Shade is the eater of time, Sara had said.

He closed the fridge and waved a kitchen towel around to disperse the foul air. As he did this, he tired quickly from his hunger and looked in the mirror next to the refrigerator. A progressed 5 o'clock shadow stretched over his jawline made up of ugly colorless hairs way too advanced to be an accurate yardstick of his time spent there. The panic started at the base of his lungs as if climbing the ladder of his ribs toward his paralyzed throat. He tried to breathe, but every breath seemed to take away more air. A low glucose heartbeat thundered in his head and felt like someone else's. He made it back to his room and fell to his knees, touching his forehead to the hardwood and begging, praying for another time slip to take him as far away as possible from the alienating fire.

Nork fought the good fight but the panic attack overwhelmed him and he lost consciousness. When he came to about an hour later, he felt better. Like a reset button was pressed in the soft folds of his brain. He ate some canned meat and decided to take a walk to loosen up.

It seemed like there were only a few sections of Sara's Cathedral Nork hadn't yet explored. His daily walks took him to many hidden nooks and rooms with purposes beyond his understanding. The only area that remained mostly unexplored was the catacombs. The rooms near the laboratory where Sara revealed to Nork the "song" supposed to save humanity from extinction. Every time Nork even approached the spiraling halls of the crypts, Sara's over-protective staff would bark warnings at him, telling him to find another place to meander. Today he would risk it. He wanted to see how deep those halls of stone would go. He would try every door to feed the beast of his curiosity and keep at least some of the boredom at bay this dreary evening.

He made his way down to the lower levels in a roundabout way, nodding to each skinny cultist as he passed trying not to look suspicious. When their white eyes lingered on him for too long, he paused and leaned against a rusty railing, pretending to rest his joints and dive deep into a counterfeit daydream. Finally, he reached the seashell-shaped hall leading down into the mausoleum vaults. There was no one to be found. Nork smiled at his luck and wasted no time. He started walking briskly from door to door, trying each handle. Every door was designed differently. Some were solid wood plated with strips of bolted iron. Some were simple sheets of reflective aluminum. One door, in particular, caught his eye during his giddy trespassing spree. It was a beautiful arch of gilded steel, covered with evenly spaced concentric squares. Each square was specially cast using bas-relief for sculpted depth. Nork realized the entire piece would have had to be forged from one huge slab of steel alloy. He put his hand against the cold surface and pushed. It gave way and the door cracked open. He stopped suddenly, surprised and excited to find the door unsecured. Summoning more courage, he pushed the door all the way open and entered the room.

It was brightly lit and looked nothing like he imagined

it would (an oily crypt filled with rotting saints). Instead, the floors were carpeted and covered in coffee stains. Folding chairs formed rows at the far end in front of a particle board podium. It looked like some kind of assembly chamber or ad hoc meditation chapel you'd find in a government building or crappy hospital. Despite its trodden municipal appearance, Nork felt a strong sense of significance to the place. He was drawn to a large display case that lined the entire right wall of the room. Behind the glass, resting on red velvet pads were hundreds of artifacts. Chips of bone, old jewelry with clouded gems, various urns. A separate section of the case contained a group of objects that piqued his curiosity. There was a bloodied shroud that held the image of a heavily bearded and beaten face. A twisted crown of spurge thorns. A chunk of ancient ship wood that was smoothed by the sea. In the center of this separate exhibit was a peculiar lump of petrified flesh. Nork took a step back and felt his intestines gurgle. An emergency was forming down there.

There's no way, he thought, laughing nervously in his head and rubbing the fresh stubble on his cheeks.

He'd heard stories about the Seeds collecting Judeo-Christian artifacts to use in their ceremonies and rituals, but this was ridiculous. Was this hideous lump really supposed to be The Holy Prepuce of Christ? Sara never did anything half-assed and this made him seriously question his doubts about the legitimacy of the relics. And just what the fuck was making his guts boil like that? He knew he'd need a bathroom soon. Just as Nork was turning around to see if there were some facilities nearby, a short old man emerged from an alcove to the left of the lectern area. Nork panicked a little at first, expecting a harsh reprimand but the man regarded him kindly and began walking toward him.

"Welcome!" the man said with a grin. He possessed a molasses Louisiana accent. "I see you've found our collection of...knick knacks. Nork, right? There's been a lot of buzz about our new Midwest visitor. I figured we'd run across each other eventually." Bob extended his frail hand in greeting. "Bob."

Nork met him in the middle with his own dead fish handshake.

"Some of these used to belong to a very important Nazarene."

Nork chuckled, "You're kidding, right? You want me to believe this is an actual ball of the foreskin from the Son of God?" Nork did not want to offend the man, but couldn't help but react to the absurdity of the situation. The last physical vestiges of an ancient religion protected in a floating cathedral at the end of the world by a man named 'Bob?'

Bob continued, "To be honest, I don't have a strong opinion either way about what you believe, Nork. But, I'm not in the habit of lying to people I've only just met." Bob went on grinning, unshakably. "I curated this exhibit myself. Many of these pieces were just lying around in the most unexpected places." Bob laughed affably at his own inside joke.

Nork exclaimed, "Jesus Christ..."

"Exactly! Did you know I found the Shroud of Turin at an abandoned dry cleaner in the Marconi Metro slums in Italy?" Bob shook his head. "The owner at least had the good sense to set it aside in his small safe before abandoning shop during the Piedmont riots." Bob sighed. "A great forgetting has happened in this world of ours."

Nork laughed again, nervously in unison with the old man. He couldn't tell if this was a joke, a dream, or both. All he knew is that he had to relieve himself badly.

"There's a fire coming, Nork. A cleansing one we've been needing for a long time. The Greeks knew it. Called it 'Apokatastasis.' When the gray world passes away, all that will be left is God. Cosmic renovation!"

"You got a bathroom around here, Bob?"

"Absolutely! Out the way you came, two doors down the hall if you hang an immediate left through that exit." Bob pointed to the massive gilded door that let Nork into the room. A flickering red 'Exit' sign hung over the small drab vestibule in front of the door. As Bob reached out his arm to point out the direction, Nork saw the tattoo of the burning heap stretched across Bob's inner forearm. The same one he swore he saw peeking out of Lesher's neckline in the HOPE© cafeteria. Gehennists. What the hell was wrong with these people?

"Thanks, Bob!" Nork smiled and shook the old man's hand one more time before waddling toward the sign, back the way he came.

On his purposeful trek to the other sacred room that was supposed to be two doors down, Nork thought of the relics resting on their velvet beds. Could they be real? Did Sara track them down across the burning world with her arcane herbs and psychotropic soul drifts? He thought of the great Jewish prophet limping to one side in Pontius's praetorium. What was the man's sense of humanity at that moment? As the mocking crown bit down into his skull? If the Christ was a symbol for our species: shunned by God, bodily outpaced by evolution, mankind's actual extinction may at least be more comfortable because of his sacrifice (like everything in the post-world age). Maybe that is the real mercy he paid for in blood at the Roman killing grounds? A soft obliteration. Our calm Archival at the hands of the Father.

Nork made it just in time to the bathroom and chose the closest stall. During his moment of relief, he took time to peruse the several scratchings on the walls of the stall partitions. More logos. More graffiti. And of course, more Gehennist symbology. The stuff was everywhere. Nork wondered how tied the Gehennists really were to The Seeds. The obvious penetration of their ideology carried bad implications. They wanted to burn the world, and Nork always thought of the Seeds as wanting the world to grow back again. The way it was, lush and full of life. This was definitely a question for Sara, Nork thought.

PLANS

"WE have to talk," Nork ventured with Sara.

Sara was with several other cultists, leaning over a table covered in blueprints. They were planning something intently. Nork recognized the name of the seed bank company on the blueprints. They must be organizing another raid.

"It'll have to wait, Nork. We're in the middle of something right now. Why don't you come back in the morning?"

Nork didn't budge, "I think it has to be now."

Sara eyed him and saw his seriousness, "Very well. Tory? Can you clean up here and give us a minute?"

The tightly woven muscle of a man nodded, scooped up the blueprints, and ushered the rest of the cultists out of Sara's chambers. Nork smelled their pungent body odor as they filed past.

Sara sat down in her chair with a peeved sigh, "How can I help you, Nork?"

"'Their worm does not die.'"

"Are you feeling OK?"

"C'mon, Sara, it's written all over your cathedral. All over the damned city. Are you leagued up with these Gehennist freaks?"

Sara sighed again and smiled patronizingly, "The Seeds have always had some affiliation with Gehennist groups. Ever since the beginning. We don't ascribe to their more extremist interpretation of The Great Change, but where our efforts can be combined, we don't hesitate to collaborate."

"For fuck's sake..."

"What's the problem, Nork?"

"Oh, I don't know, maybe just that you happened to be allied with a widespread terrorist organization that wants to scorch the surface of planet earth. No big deal."

"It's all empty rhetoric, Nork. Like television evangelism. They want essentially the same thing as we do. A world that's changed."

"I can't believe your deluding yourself like this."

Sara interrupted, a little irate, "In spite of their 'colorful' mythology, they're useful to me, Nork. I don't concern myself with their ridiculous apocalypse predictions or their worship of Phoenician demigods, and neither should you. But I do need their numbers. If we're to rebuild the world of men, I'm afraid we'll have to coexist with some of the fanatics. These times breed them like flies."

Sara sipped her steaming drink and looked at Nork with raised eyebrows.

Nork shook his head, "You're playing with fire, Sara. These people will not hesitate to destroy and kill anything that threatens their vision of their divine catastrophe. They don't believe in humanity like you. It's not about healthy babies and pretty gardens. It's about self-immolation and screeching flames."

"I have it under control, Nork. And if you're done telling me how to lead my people, I need to get back to work."

"Sacking another seed library, huh?"

Sara smiled again, this time revealing more of her irritation: "Yes, in fact. Why? You wanna come along?"

Nork blurted, not really thinking it through, "Sure. When do we start?"

"Hilarious. You'd freeze up faster in the field than a boy soldier with a toy gun, Nork. Admit it."

"So, you'll risk allying with a worldwide coalition of suicidal maniacs, but you won't let me tag along on one of your little 'outings?' I can handle myself."

"Going a little stir-crazy, are we?"

Sara was right. Nork realized he was upset and being impulsive, but he really did want to attend the raid. Anything to step out of this pollen-infested sink drain for a few hours.

"Fine. If it will appease you, I'll let you come. But I'm going to have Tory follow you like a dog and I'm not responsible for what happens if you get hurt," Sara finally conceded.

"I look forward to it." Nork's angry adrenaline was starting to concede to anxiety and dread.

"We leave in the morning. Before the sun. Get some sleep."

EXIT

NORK could not stop pacing around his room. It was early morning, about 40 minutes until sunrise. He regretted the decision to attend the raid with Sara's soldiers but knew there was no turning back now. Chickening out would make him even more anxious. He wondered if they would give him a gun or some kind of weapon. Probably not, he thought. Sara obviously didn't put much stake in his martial capabilities. He would basically be a nuisance. A tourist. A photojournalist without a notepad or camera bumbling onto the battlefield. He knew the sperm and egg repositories were heavily guarded electronic fortresses watched by well-armed private security firms. He didn't know whether Sara was killing these people to take her product or just incapacitating them somehow. The operation struck him as more of a stealth mission than anything, but anything could happen. Anything could go wrong when heisting expensive biological material from men with tactical assault rifles.

A harsh knocking came from his door.

"Nork. Ready?" It was Tory's voice. Scratched and groggy.

"Coming," Nork mumbled.

Nork followed Tory through the hall and down the stairwell to meet the others mustering in the arboretum. Nork looked around and saw no one carrying firearms. He didn't know whether to find this comforting or unnerving.

Tory, at least, had a 6-inch sheathed knife fixed to his belt. Nork was starting to lose his nerve. The familiar red rose of panic was starting to bud inside his heart. As his breathing quickened and he started to feel numb in his hands, Sara entered the gardens from the spiraling halls leading out of the catacombs. Nork's blood was pumping and, in his agitation, he also found himself incredibly aroused by Sara's appearance. Her leather pants and tattered men's size V-neck fit her body well, making her look more feminine and powerful than Nork had ever seen. Her face was streaked with dirt, crushed plant pigment, or shoe polish or something. He tried not to ogle.

Sara walked up to him, acutely aware of Nork's nervous effort to hide his attraction. "Are you prepared for this?" She smirked a little behind her shaded face. She smelled like sweat and grass.

Nork nodded with an uncomfortable half-smile that just barely involved a few small muscles at the creases of his cheeks.

"Let's go," commanded Sara.

They left the cathedral before Nork could catch his breath. The chants and spirited yells that echoed through the narthex ceased the moment the doors opened on the city still dark. Sara led the brigade, motioning silently with her hands and keeping an accurate count with her drastically white eyes. They flooded into the streets, keeping close to the walls of the buildings as they passed, bearing in some direction unknown to Nork but where he guessed stood an impenetrable bank made of steel and filled with semen. The requirement to keep up with Sara's little strike team didn't give him much time to panic, but he was still more scared than he could ever remember being. He could feel the blast of Tory's breath on his back. It smelled of rotten apples and root vegetables.

Nork was tired before the trek even begun and his energy was fading fast. He couldn't keep up with these paleolithic athletes. Tory pushed him gently every time Nork started lagging behind. Finally, they came to a staging point a couple of blocks from the seed bank and stopped.

Nork laughed through desperate puffs of air, "That's all...you got?"

Sara snapped, "SHUT UP!"

Something was wrong. Sara gave several hand signals to her team that Nork didn't understand and found kind of silly. It reminded Nork of baseball, that old American mainstay that disappeared along with all the other commercial sports. People just couldn't do them anymore.

He looked around, trying to determine what the problem was. He stood up and that's when he saw the trio of armed guards walking toward their position from the street closest to the seed bank entrance. Tory grasped Nork's left shoulder and tore him down to the ground. Nork felt pain shoot up his neck and thought seriously that his arm may be out of socket.

Urgently Tory commanded, "Lay the fuck down and be silent!"

Nork obeyed. His heart was beating furiously now as the reality of the situation sank in. They were pinned down in both directions, guards also closing in from the rear. They must have heard the approach of Sara's team and begun tracking them. Sara looked stern and a little rattled. Nork could see her improvising a plan in her brain as her eyes flitted from object to object around her. Nork hugged the pavement as closely as he could powerlessly waiting to see what would happen next.

After enough silence passed by to make Nork willing to lift his head, gunfire broke out from behind a parked car ahead of their position. Twin pinwheels of fire flashed from the hands of two dark figures dressed like goggled shock troops. The bullets slammed into the concrete above Nork's head scattering Sara's fighters into the various features of the street. Some took cover behind dumpsters and cars. Others took bullets and fell to the ground pouring red.

Nork was paralyzed. He could feel his body trying to crawl in spite of him, but he felt like he was going nowhere. He could hear Tory screaming at him from behind a protective corner of the building they were up against a moment ago. All Nork could make out was "STAY DOWN!" Nork couldn't have stood up if he wanted to. He managed to roll over to the edge of the curb and looked instinctively around for Sara. She was nowhere in sight and he considered this a relief. Nork saw that some of her soldiers circled to flank the attack and cut the throats of at least three seed bank guards, but the "ratatat" of gunfire continued. Nork was slowly becoming more in charge of his body. He looked down and saw a storm drain entrance a couple of feet in front of him. Without thinking he launched himself forward, ignoring Tory's yells, and slid under the grate. He splashed into a fouling-smelling darkness.

Nork emerged from the sewer covered in the united shit of New York City. For a while, he wasn't convinced he would make it out alive. The sewer tunnels were labyrinthine, acrid, and dark. The hidden intestines of America's grandest metropolis. Nork made a mental note to grab a handful of doxycycline samples from the HOPE© break room after he got back to Illinois. That's where he was headed, he decided. New York was bending his mind in strange directions. He didn't know what to believe anymore about Sara, about anything. He needed to talk to Dolden. His best friend would ground him. Home would put his feet back on solid ground.

Nork's subway ride down to New York Level 1 was embarrassing. His stench basically emptied the subway car of people, which he appreciated because it gave him a chance to think. He planned to find a cheap motel down in the fogs, wash up, take account of his remaining cash and find a bus back to Fraternity.

The bus ride was long and Nork could not sleep. Every hour his buttocks would spasm with pain and his calves would cramp and tighten beyond his control. He just continued to sit, mind accelerating beyond the bus and arriving home far ahead of the rest of his body. When the bus finally arrived at the Fraternity metropolitan station, it was a uniting. His brain had been waiting for him there for hours.

He went home first to the apartment he had rented on the south side of the city. The basket of rent money he left for the landlord before his New York adventure was depleted. The place stunk of neglect. The kind of emptiness that gets filled by mold and small creatures that seek places where they won't be bothered by the bi-pedal giants that roam the earth. He walked to his bedroom and collapsed on the bed letting the plume of dust settle onto his skin like blonde snow. Tomorrow, he would see Dolden and hopefully rescue some shards of the last two years. He didn't even think much about Sara. Whether she was dead or alive. His care was buried beneath a strong sense of betrayal. Something in him knew that she was still breathing. Still casting her psychic nets into distant realms. Exploring the bottoms of the oceans and the pull of secret stars.

He closed his eyes and slept.

Nork was nervous walking into HOPE© the next day. He knew no one would recognize him in the receiving area. But as soon as the elevators opened on his department office. There would be gasps, looks, and judgments. Security would escort him out as soon as they clocked him on the cameras, but he only needed to be there long enough to reach Dolden. Set up some time to talk.

As the elevators parted their steel teeth, Nork slinked out and made a beeline to Dolden's Biomed offices. On his way down the hall, he spotted one of the Death Peckers exiting the bathrooms. Nork gave him a sarcastic smile and watched the face of his former boss swell red. Nork continued and rushed through the crowds of Biomed engineers chattering in their own special language. He came to Dolden's office and knocked aggressively adrenaline pumping.

"Come in, whoever it is...(*Christ*)," exclaimed a very much surprised Dolden!

Nork opened the door and stepped inside. Dolden's office was a disaster site of documents and scientific equipment. It smelled like vinegar and formaldehyde. Dolden was obviously stressed out and hunched at his desk scribbling notes furiously on graph paper.

"Dolden," replied Nork calmly.

Dolden looked up to see his friend.

"Nork!" Dolden returned with a wide smile.

"Still stinks like hell in here."

"Yeah, I like to keep it nice and foul. Keeps the interns away. It's good to see you, Nork."

"You, too."

There was a pause of silence between the two friends that seemed to last an awkward eternity.

"Listen, Nork, I don't think you have much time. There are a lot of rumors around here about what you've been up to the last two years. They're concerned about your...recent affiliations."

"I figured as much. We need to find a time to talk."

Dolden stood up and anxiously gathered his papers into a stack. Nork noticed the approach of three HOPE© security officers on the camera monitors above Dolden's workstation.

Dolden murmured, "My house. Tonight."

The guards burst in like bulls.

"Tsk, tsk. Where are your manners, people? This is a place of science for fuck's sake!" Dolden shook his fist in the air sarcastically and grinned with mischief.

Ignoring Dolden, a guard stared at Nork. "Mr. Nork, you'll come with us."

"Right," capitulated Nork.

Nork was escorted out of HOPE© probably, he thought, for the last time. As they passed the cafeteria, Nork caught eyes with Lesher Fixtrue devouring some unappetizing slice of beetle shell quiche. Lesher stared at Nork oddly as they passed and just before disappearing past the mess hall entrance, he noticed Lesher smile at him strangely.

At 8 pm on a Friday, Nork left his apartment. It was "August" according to his calendar and the air was tipped just over the edge of the golden hour. The orange light swirled around him like flames as he walked with his right arm over his eyes, aiming himself toward the park trail that led to Dolden's neighborhood. After some distance, his vision finally adjusted and he took in the full force of the burning light. The sun always seemed like it was getting closer and closer. Was it the sun? Or was it the earth? Drawn toward the blaze like a fanatical moth? Either way, the light sprayed false importance into strange thoughts as he entered the park. Thoughts that were not words but sounds. Unnerving gibberish. The same nonsensical shouting that filled him before on his drive out of Fraternity toward New York and the near death of his mind.

By the time he made it to Dolden's door, the sunset was less intense and the unbearable noise died down to a whisper that would stay throughout the evening. Maybe it was always there, and just got drowned out when he left the private circle of his own silence.

Before Nork sat down on the Mastre's porch and poured himself a mug of Dolden's barley-ed poison, Dolden had already dived into monologue. Nork prepared himself to be seated for a while at Dolden's pulpit of despair.

"Sorry, we had to cut it so short today at the office, Nork. You understand."

"Yeah, no, I probably shouldn't have even gone. I just...wanted to talk in person."

"Of course. A lot's happened since you've been away. I've been watching the world's slow boring collapse for a while now, progressing every day. Now it's accelerating in an arc toward the sun."

Nork wasn't fully sure what Dolden was on about, but he wanted him to finish.

"Your department of whores continue to sell mass suicide disguised as social unity to a vulnerable world. I gotta piss." Dolden stood up for a trip to the bathroom. Nork waited, intrigued. Dolden always had to be decoded, but Nork was convinced it was worth the effort.

Dolden exited the bathroom in a characteristic explosion of force. The toilet was still singing lamentations behind him as he wagged purple disinfectant off his hands.

Dolden continued, "So, how do you make the whole world fall down?"

Nork thought and couldn't find the answer Dolden was looking for. "You tell me," he said a little more mockingly than he intended.

Dolden answered intentionally, "Unify the masses, build civilization toward the sky, and after all, eggs are tucked away in one tall and seemingly impregnable basket, tear it down. But you need a strong push, something that can dissolve the entire foundation. You basically need to implode it from the inside out. Meaning you need to understand its most fundamental building blocks. You need to find that one common element, that one universal sentence that can be unwritten."

Nork pictured the symphony of ripples displayed on Sara's lab monitors, what her Seeds cult so cryptically called 'The Song'. He wondered whether to tell Dolden that Sara had already figured it all out (kind of) and that his work at HOPE© was now probably redundant and/or dangerous.

"DNA," Nork answered as he reached back to another lengthy Dolden session about genetics.

"Well, yes, but more specifically the language that DNA is written in. The language of our cosmic instructions.

Learn those rules, or at least grasp how they essentially work and you can either fortify or destroy all human life."

Nork carefully continued his verbal staccato not wishing to interrupt Dolden's rhythm, "HOPE©."

Dolden continued, "Right. The words written inside all men are finally becoming intelligible. The language that has been alive inside us since the beginning is becoming known, and we find that it is full of instructions. I've seen what the instructions are now saying, and they are telling us very specifically to 'let go'. I watch 100 test subjects die every week behind Lexan glass. I pump their murky veins with priceless micro-technological wonders, and I watch their bodies reject them. One after the other. Handshakes, release forms, hopeful eyes, morgue dispositions. It's draining, even for a sociopath like me. What's even more draining is the fact that nano-technology didn't usher in the 'next wave of *human* evolution' like all the med columnists and Big Pharma analysts promised. It's time to admit that it failed to supplant this crap flesh we inherited from mother earth. It failed science, Nork, like a lost ticket to godhood. A blown chance to show the universe once and for all that WE can do it better. That the human is ready to take his own life into his hands. And now we're all standing around in the lab knee-deep in corpses, wondering what the fuck happened? Instead of a cure facility, we have a hospice and a massive R&D paradigm shift. And HOPE© couldn't care less. I waste my work days now helping find ways to keep this society of mutants and degenerates alive long enough before Archival to host a profitable addiction to HOPE©'s healthcare solutions: the consolation prizes to the world. Honorable mention medals awarded at the immortality science fair. And here's the problem, everyone seems completely fine with this business model. Probably for a long list of justifications, all of them spun by you Global Messaging savants as altruistic deathbeds with clean sheets and fluffy pillows. It's not good enough, though. We're fucking dying. And no one gives a blue shit."

Dolden continued, "It's HOPE©. HOPE© is the thrust of this morbid unification. This spirit that whispers 'build the tower' and 'fall asleep.' It makes sense to people, they nod, and they heft hammers in their palms to build the tower. The tower they believe is the only forward path besides illness and decay. So, let's pool the resources, and build it tall. Pierce the sky, so we can see heaven one last time."

Nork searched for something to say. "Well, HOPE© *has* added what basically amounts to elective global genocide to its 10-year plan."

Dolden countered, "Archival isn't the end, Nork, and I wouldn't call it genocide. Some novel form of bodily euthanasia, maybe. But no one really knows what haunted digital landscapes we'll have to wander in those machines. What mind will be like without body. So, in a sense, I guess you're right. It is a brand-new kind of death we've invented."

Nork added sarcastically, "Ah, to be violently ripped from my body by some software-based psychopomp. We truly are blessed."

Nork searched inside his weakened heart to see if enough belief in the species still resided there. Was it worth telling Dolden about Sara and her discovery? Her muddy ties to the Gehennist extremists? "THEIR WORM DOES NOT DIE." Each time he tried to visualize himself informing Dolden, it was like acting something out in a dream and waking up each time to complete paralysis. Something inside stopped him and he had no idea where the mental obstacle came from.

In desperate tones, Dolden continued, "Suffering Call to Unity Homogenization Apocalypse Replacement. It's a path, a logic that expresses itself through our species. Those bat-shit Gehennists are ready to burn the world down to the ground. HOPE© and its visionaries, its kings and its pawns…you, me, we are just tools, half-aware if aware at all. The universe is preparing us for removal. With the profit margins HOPE© has seen over the last 15 years, both our departments should be as powerful by now as European governments. But all the money is going into my Lifeboat. Into our replacements." Dolden thought of Origen who was probably back at the lab, working tirelessly into the night. Did he hate his own son? "We will be filed for good."

Nork swallowed inside his dry mouth. He despised feeling like going back to the time-thieving dream of Sara's Cathedral was his only hope for survival. He didn't feel comfortable there amongst the odd men and fecund gardens.

Nork replied, "You said Lifeboat failed."

"I said I failed, Nork. I failed to make it into what it should have been. Our great miracle. The ark of humanity. Instead, it will be our children that destroy us. What's weird is that our new children more resemble our parents. The neo-human in all of its grace and glory will tuck us into the libraries where we'll all become novels too long and unremarkable for anyone to read."

"So, you did it? It works?" Nork exclaimed. *Not nearly as well as...wait. Wet green compost filled his mind's eye. Was that his thought?*

Dolden solemnly answered, "It works for them. Not for us. We are going away, Nork. Soon we will all be sick and inside the same borders. Territories are already being consolidated as countries cash in their sovereignty and independence for the healthcare only HOPE© can provide. It's funny. Chaos, division, war, and revolution are the only actions that can bring about the necessary conditions for our survival. These are the only things that have a chance of saving our crippled species, and we of course want nothing to do with them. At least the Gehenna cultists are fighting. The rest of us are presented with our last hope against the annihilating comforts offered by our neo-human concierges, and we just want to sleep because we already lost our taste for the lust and pain life requires to keep swinging. Every time I think about the dying hive of disease our species has become; I see life itself committing suicide inside us. Because deep down in the genetic core of our being, none of us really want to be here while this is happening. Religions have assembled to carry out their agendas of doom. Nations are gradually surrendering their aspirations. 'Worldliness' is way out of style. And so, death spreads sympathetically, like a yawn. At this point, most people, most groaning blobs of inflammation would rather throw the dice on the 'next world' than maintain belief in what's right in front of them. But who can blame them? This planet is bald and cancerous and so are we. The depression, the drug abuse, the occult ritual poisonings, the pandemic of suicides are all overkill. Our bodies, our code, and life itself is administering our euthanasia. And it's an act of mercy really. Just look around."

FIRE AND WATER

AT 5:30 AM on a Sunday morning, a short man named Bob exited the doors of Sara's Cathedral. The smile on his face was wide in the morning light. He aimed his eyes toward the incendiary clouds in the east beyond the darkened buildings as if the color and smoke were some opener for a much larger and more raucous display. What Bob knew, and mostly orchestrated himself through the proper channels, was that massive charges of propellant napalm were set to ignite across the entire city in approximately 12 minutes. During the routine repository raids over the last several months, the Gehennists among Sara's ranks had rigged an astonishingly large number of buildings across New York Levels 1 and 2 against her knowledge. Not even the Cathedral was spared. The cavernous foundations of the old skyscraper it was stuck to were wrapped in enough napalm to incinerate everything within a half-mile radius. The Cathedral would be the epicenter. The opening act that would spread The Cleanse through the forsaken city like a great sizzling flood. Apokatastasis at last. By the end of this grand show, Bob thought, the only soul left to survey the mess would be God. He would hover over the waters and rubble just like he'd done in the days of old, and he would be pleased.

Six minutes.

In the upper floors of the Cathedral, Sara and the rest of her cultists slept in peace. Some Gehennists privy to the plan watched out their windows in the dark, awaiting their magnificent end. Bob was disappointed that the relics had to be destroyed, too, but God told him it was necessary. The Divine Maker said they were simply crude material leftovers of work He accomplished a long time ago. He had no more use for them. This saddened Bob, to hear the Master of the Universe shrug off Bob's entire life's work. But who was Bob to question The Lord of Lords? The relics belonged to history, not to Bob. And history was about to engulf us all. So, Bob dumped them onto the cobbled stone, soaked them in gasoline, and burned them to the ground, trying to hold back the tears. He watched as the Foreskin of Christ curled up like newspaper kindling and disappeared forever.

Two minutes.

Not long now, Bob thought as he sat down next to a statue of a placid woman with face downturned. Her name was Mary and Bob was one of the only people who remembered this. The Mother of Christ would be his companion for God's orange blazing fanfare. Bob was not politically ambitious by any means, but he hoped he would receive some kind of special status in heaven after all this was over. After all, he was the mastermind behind the destruction of an entire evil city. Paver of the way to a washed City of God. That had to be worth something more than just a pat on the back from The Big Guy. He would see.

One minute.

He took one last long look at the Cathedral, his home for 45 years. A sharp but brittle spike of remorse rose up from under his ribs as he thought of the relics and the other faithful Seeds he betrayed. Not to mention Sara, who allowed him the freedom to accomplish such a rarified collection of the scraps of God. Necessary sacrifices for the grand design, he decided. Besides, who would miss their own lives after they're dead anyway? The hard part is always only the countdown, and that would be over very soon.

Before Bob could reach the end of this stream of thought, a fiery plume swallowed the cathedral and everything around it, disintegrating into ash Bob and everyone else in Sara's tall Cathedral of Clouds.

FIRE WATER

DOLDEN wasn't fully sure whether he remembered his keycard as he approached the airlock doors leading into a dark and vacant HOPE© prick. It was way before working hours, and he was drunk. He slapped his back pocket and smiled as he felt his badge. Entrance would be granted on this premature morning.

He staggered through the empty receiving area, his drunkenness providing just the amount of privacy he needed from his diamond-cutting mind. Smirking at the elevator, he decided to take the stairs to his office area instead. Because, hell, if the stairs could do the job first.

The hinged door leading from the staircase exploded with a huffing Dolden. He grunted and crashed down to the carpet for what seemed to him like the last desperate heartbeats of life. They felt fast and far beyond him. Pale orange street light from the surrounding business complex covered half his face. The illuminated section of his cheeks seemed to swell and burn as he watched it in the mirror of the office glass. He picked himself up and continued his stupefied trudge to his office which was connected to the whole laboratory stack like an arm of lightning.

His smashing down into the ergonomic chair semi-crucified his sagging body in a way that forced his shoulders up and convinced him that this was the last place he would rest his sacred bones. He opened a cherry wood drawer on a

.357 revolver. Before reaching for the gun, his eyes caught on a prototype consciousness transfer network still lying on his desk. His mind immediately prioritized spontaneous death-orgasm over the other great mystery hiding within the darkness of the .357 barrel. Dolden was infinitely logical to the end. Pleasure meant more than pain. He would thrust his consciousness into a corrupt drive. Into a 65-pin emptiness that would simultaneously drain his loins as well as his living soul. He strapped the thing around his head, plugged the end cable into a defunct storage unit, and looked one last time at the lights outside the office windows. They seemed to dance like stars. Fires that would keep burning for a very long time even without him.

"Dad?" A familiar voice sounded from behind him, an exact replica of his own emitting from Origen's cloned throat.

Dolden turned in his chair. Origen was standing in the shadows cast by the growth chambers.

The clone trotted over to his dad and sat on Dolden's lap.

"What are you doing here so early, huh?" Dolden asked. Dolden's heavy exhalations bristled with alcohol vapor.

"Just running some routines on the next brood, like you said," dutifully replied Origen.

"Good...good, good."

"Is everything OK, dad?"

Dolden furrowed his brow to let out a belch, then

smiled far into the distance: "It absolutely is. Hey, I want you to know something."

Origen giggled, "You stink, dad!"

Dolden laughed and playfully blew foul air into Origen's face. "DO I? Do I stink, son? Please tell me if my breath stinks, I have a hot date today!"

Origen continued to squirm in his father's lap, laughing like a child though his body was already adult-sized and fully grown. Dolden still referred to him as his "little guy" even though the growth stimulants definitely served their purpose.

Finally, Origen asked, "Why do you have that thing on your head?"

"This thing? Why? Don't you like it?" Dolden poked his son's ribs. "I'm considering making it a permanent addition to my wardrobe. What do you think, little guy?"

Origen shrugged, still laughing off some of the tickling.

Dolden continued, "Hey, I want to tell you something."

"What, dad?"

Dolden held his clone's head close to his, kissing his offspring above the ear. "You are the single most powerful thing I ever did with my life."

Origen was quiet.

Dolden asked, "I need you to do something for me, OK?"

Dolden handed the transfer machine controls to his

son, flipping up the protective plastic that covered the kill switch with his thumb like a Zippo lighter. He knew what would happen with Origen's fingerprints left on the button. There would be a company-wide investigation. *The Lion must sometimes devour his children.*

Dolden continued, "In 30 seconds, I need you to press this button."

Origen laughed, "Why? What is this?"

"Just a test. It's an experimental deep sleep unit I've been tampering with. Uses the same basic technology as a transfer network. I figured I'd tinker a bit before work. You wanna help me out?" Dolden carefully concealed the corrupted hard drive and the wires connecting to it in his coat pocket.

"It's not going to hurt you, is it?" a concerned Origen asked.

"No, it's not going to hurt."

"And I wake you up right after, right?"

"Of course."

"30 seconds?"

Dolden joked in a deep voice, "30 seconds. BEGIN THE COUNTDOWN!"

That half-minute drizzled by slowly for Dolden like a light rain as he held his firstborn clone in his hairy arms listening to Origen's voice count out the last remaining moments of his father's peculiar life. Dolden just rocked his overgrown son back and forth in his lap, looking farther and farther away into that distance ahead of him.

An innocent red button was pressed, and all that was left of Dolden, other than his growing family of Nex and responsibility for shelving away the entire human race, was a whitish drip to the floor containing millions that died in their own over-crowded ocean before they ever had a clue where to swim.

ARCHIVaL

NORK could feel Sara's death like an absence of air. Dolden's demise paled in comparison. But like the fire that now raged over the waters of New York, both losses sucked his breath straight from his lungs. Nork's friends invaded his mind, beautifully ruined it in so many ways, and now that they were gone, so was he.

The Nex treated Nork well despite his known affiliations with Sara's cause. Maybe there was some shred of the real Dolden written in them somewhere, a spark of inborn sympathy sparing him from a holding cell or worse. The Nex neo-humans seemed to understand the old humanity patiently, like a mother coaxing anxiety out of her children. Nork couldn't help but be infuriated by their decency. Each androgynous Dolden-faced being was an enlightened shepherd. Profoundly reasonable. Attentive and accommodating, regarding humanity with respect but also a humorous condescension. People were like dying old men, refusing their plates of food, shitting their gowns, and spewing epitaphs at hospice nurses. But in the face of all the hate and wonder and petulance the Nex stayed sage. Nork was even able to keep his apartment until the scheduled time of his archiving that he was able to choose on his own. Nork thought it would be easier to process everything if Lifeboat had been a violent coup of homicidal clones. Instead, the city was calm, the Cult of Gehenna was splintered and gone, the sun rose and set on the same bright chariot's path, and Sara the Healer was dead.

The three months before his archival passed much like they did at the Cathedral. Where others whiled the time away with family or checked off miscellanies on their bucket lists, Nork took the time to think. Nothing too heavy. Not why he was here, or what purpose he served as an audience member in this slow play that was finally approaching final applause. Instead, he thought about people. Not just the few that were close to him, but everyone. The whole of old humanity. Their faces, skin, and breath became one giant gross and beautiful spill. And while he was thinking, stuck to a park bench or staring out as far as he could into the gray outside the many windows of his small silly life, what ultimately flowered in his heart was laughter.

On his chosen day, he joined the crowd that was forming outside the Memory Archives building closest to his street. A gentle-faced Dolden clone approached him humbly.

"Good morning, sir!" It said in a soothing tone.

Nork nodded and gave a nervous half-grin to the polite simulacrum of his dead best friend.

"If you don't mind exposing your shoulder, sir, we have your pre-meds prepared."

Nork complied and felt a light bee sting in the meat of his right shoulder. Almost immediately the morning's anxiety submerged. In the theater of his mind, pure blue water poured in from every emergency exit, drowning each screaming audience member. Nork smiled as the hounding voices gargled and ceased. He joined the rest of the happy people in line. Lively chatter and coffee steam drifted over the masses. Some people laughed in small circles of friends as they ate one last warm breakfast together. As he waited in line with them, he felt golden. He chatted with a few strangers, making small talk and enjoying it for the first time in his life. When the conversation died down in direct proportion to his distance from the marble stairs, he remembered some words from Dolden:

"*This is reality, Nork. Nothing big or miraculous ever happens quickly. The violence of miracles, the explosiveness of large world-shaping events are tall tales ripped out of history as soon as they are old enough to be first forgotten.*"

Nork hadn't really understood those words when he heard them, or when he pondered them while circling the hardwood floor of his sun-drenched room in Sara's Cathedral. His chest ached a little in his throat when he thought about how much time actually passed during his stay at New York Level 2. It seemed so impossible. The vengeful Shade detox both expanded and collapsed the last remnants of his life. The birth and death of his entire universe was contained within what now felt like a single instant of being thrillingly afraid of Sara's eyes. Yet the longer he considered it, the smaller his regret became. At least he was able to spend his own personal slice of eternity in the presence of her. Maybe that was just the right amount of love he would ever allow himself in this life.

In the archival room, some Nex clones helped Nork into the transfer apparatus. Hundreds of others waited in their machines around him. Each face flashed with excitement as if all of this were a theme park ride ready to blast them into space on an orgasmic rainbow.

The last step in the seating procedure involved strapping an antiseptic saddle around Nork's genitals. Nork guessed correctly at its purpose and laughed to himself as the nice little clones fondled his pubic area. He would leave something behind after all.

"Are you ready, sir?" A kind, surprisingly female voice sounded over the com system above his seat. He turned his head to look at the command center window. A tall feminine Dolden clone manned the controls. Nork would have been far more perturbed by this final sight if it weren't for the magical pre-meds still turning his brain into an ocean. Nork nodded, not really sure and not really caring whether they could see his gesture. He was already so far away amidst the drowning waves.

Once everyone was properly seated, the helper Nex left the room through sliding doors. The Dolden-lady behind the glass pressed a button and Nork launched back, drifting inside his head to the small forgotten barn in the reeds upstate that completely by chance became a sarcophagus for as many of him as there are stars. He remembered seeing the place from across a field of dead grass a mile or so away from the train station, and thinking to himself how tiny things can seem until you're inside them. The chill air told him it was the end of summer already, and time to die. Again. That was the price of that delicate and over-serious age. You had to die many times. One of his older caretakers once told him that there are no real endings, that the universe is infinite and simply has none. This was wrong, he always thought. The universe is made of endings.

And that's why he had to die. Every day, every semester, every year. With each ending. He thought of it as he pushed useless death out of the center of his teenage waist, sweating private wasteful sweat in the frustrated heat of those lonesome days. He thought about everyone during these moments. When his mind was cut open and spilling out on a movie screen above the barn where no one could see the bare shoulders of a beautiful bright-eyed girl he thought he would know forever. In that moment, as the Archival scanners purpled behind his closed eyelids, Sara's skin only meant as much to him as it was part of the rest of the swirl. The tastes, the faces, and the sky's light painted differently by each circling season. Always changing. Always dying.

And so, he let his head fall back and felt the weight of his swollen tongue. His closed eyes threw a black protective cape around him, and his hands grew warm and then cold as he felt overflow and the emptiness that followed. No course to consider what a stranger he was to himself when the feeling in his flesh was gone. With his last thoughts hovering in his physical brain, he visualized that all-encompassing screen. All the people. The globs of light in space. What was left of them after the dream ends and can no longer keep the spectacle intact? A disappearing pool that leaves a map in the dust to where it all begins again and again.

SOUNDTRACK

In addition to writing, James W. Yates was passionate about music. While creating "Nork and the End," he composed an album of songs meant to act as the soundtrack to the novel. The album is entitled "Phantom Arum," and is believed to be an allusion to the brief lifespan of humanity in relation to the universe. You can listen to that soundtrack by typing the address below and searching for the "Phantom Arum" album.

https://soundcloud.com/jim-yates

A PORTION OF THE PROCEEDS FROM THIS BOOK WILL CONTRIBUTE TO THE JAMES W. YATES ENDOWED SCHOLARSHIP

Class of 2009 This scholarship honors the legacy of James W. Yates and seeks to inspire recipients with the story of his character and accomplishments. Jim was passionate about ideas, philosophy, and writing. He started a Philosophy Club while in high school. He was a deep thinker known for spirited discussions and debates punctuated with his trenchant wit. Jim was funny, humble, curious, loyal, and approachable. He enjoyed developing relationships with fellow students and faculty members. Jim initiated a themed residential community at the Hanover College Young House featuring regular informal social gatherings with a hosted Hanover professor. These were memorable moments for students and professors to get to know one another as people and to allow topics and discussions to evolve

freely. Among his many fulfilling experiences while a student at Hanover was studying abroad in Belgium and getting to explore the history and culture of Europe. His adventures made us frequently wonder, "Where in the world is Jim Yates?" Throughout his career at Hanover College, Jim was on the Dean's List and was inducted in the Alpha Lambda Delta Academic Fraternity for his academic achievements. Jim satisfied his creative energies through sound engineering, music and writing. He earned prestigious core and advanced certifications in audio engineering and sound production at The Recording Workshop School of

Audio Engineering and Production in Chillicothe, Ohio. He opened his own sound studio as an avocation, mixed the recordings of several bands and recorded his own original works. Jim also wrote a novel (as yet unpublished) that addressed many of the social justice struggles he observed in the American healthcare system, society, and commerce. Jim was an outdoorsman and explorer. Happy Valley was a natural haven for escape and rejuvenation. It was a local expression of his life-long love of forests and the wilderness. At age 15 he became a registered "Forty-Sixer," having completed climbs to the summits of all 46 high peaks in the Adirondack Mountains of New York. He hiked the historic Northville-Lake Placid Trail, also in New York. Together with a friend from

Hanover, he through-hiked the Knobstone Trail in the backcountry of southern Indiana. And he joined a three-week expedition to The Grand Canyon sponsored by Hanover. All told, Jim hiked nearly a thousand miles of remote and rugged terrain and traversed nearly a quarter of a million feet of elevation changes. Jim Yates's story is inspiring not so much because he accomplished all these things but because he did so while facing years of intense suffering. He was never one to complain. He embraced life to the fullest with his unique

sense of humor and playfulness. He loved his friends, his professors, his studies and he loved Hanover – the best years of his life, he would say. Jim Yates embodied perseverance and resilience. He was admired by his teachers and professors. And he was cherished by his family and many friends. Jim died soon after his 30th birthday from complications of Lupus and Crohn's Disease – conditions he battled since childhood. He is buried in upstate New York, at the foot of the first mountain he climbed as a young boy. He often said that he hoped other students would taste the joy he experienced at Hanover and benefit from such an excellent education.